The Battle For Freedom

**Praxton
Book 2**

N. S. Howard

Published by
Melange Books, LLC
White Bear Lake, MN 55110
www.melange-books.com

Cover Art by Lynsee Lauritsen

Prologue

With the spread of humanity throughout the galaxy, a series of independent planetary societies evolved. This was made possible by the discovery of a space warping method, which allowed instant travel, though at great cost. The need for trade led to the formation of the Sol Alliance, at first only within the solar system, but later, under the title of the Alliance, throughout the known Galaxy.

The Charter of Conduct:

The Charter of Conduct, heavily promoted by Earth, but widely accepted among the planets adhering to the Alliance, spelled out what constituted acceptable society in terms of laws and social behaviour. Besides the Charter of Conduct, each Associated World was allowed to send a number of members—determined by population and gross trade with Sol—to the Alliance's elected legislature. Membership came with a price, and some worlds felt the cost to join the Alliance was unreasonably high. However, to agree to the Charter of Conduct and not join the Alliance was risky, as everyone wanted a say in the Charter. And not to sign the Charter was akin to hiding a dark secret.

Eventually, an overwhelming number of inhabited planets signed up to join the Alliance. The alternative was to be taken over by force.

The Charter of Conduct Office became a large organization, forcing even the Alliance government to change laws to suit the huge bureaucracy. Very few people claimed to understand every aspect of the complex Charter, and many of its clauses had to be argued out in court for exact interpretation of content. The Charter of Conduct Office employed more people than the total population of some of the smaller worlds and its influence was felt everywhere.

Praxton

Praxton is slightly larger than Earth and resides in an orbit around a reddish coloured star larger than the Earth's sun. To compensate, Praxton is slightly further away from its star than the Earth is from the Sun.

Praxton is almost half land mass versus water and much of the world consists of large desert areas. The soil is reddish in colour, but has enough nutrients to support agriculture. Overall, the temperature on the planet is warm, with only small cool Polar Regions. From a distance Praxton, looks like an oversized Mars with oceans.

Two separate groups arrived at planetary orbit within days of each other and founded Praxton in the year 2315 CE. One group was a Ukrainian consortium interested in developing Praxton for farming and mining of minerals. Most of this group were military personnel. The second group was a privately owned pilgrim ship financed by the Arab-Christian Council. The council was initially put together to promote harmony between people living in the middle east of old Earth. Over the years, the council became involved in financing pilgrim ships, specifically ones promoting their cultural beliefs.

The Arab and Christian components were both wealthy, had conservative viewpoints and wanted to export those beliefs. There was a trade off on some beliefs between the two factions, though both groups believed the male to be head of the household. The Arabs accepted that women could wear as much or as little as they chose, while the Christians accepted the Arab premise that a man could have more than one wife.

The Ukrainian group had a shortage of women and discovered quickly the Arab-Christian group had an abundance of women. The Ukrainian group were at a disadvantage as far as trying to increase the population of Praxton but being military people, decided taking over Praxton and possessing all the women, might be possible. There were a number of skirmishes, most of them initiated by the Ukrainian group. The war didn't last long; neither group could afford the resources for any sustained conflict. The two factions came to an agreement and decided on a combination of an elected military style of government.

The creation of the new regime did not end the lawlessness on

Praxton. The population was spread over a large area and consisted of farms and small towns, making it possible for raiders to operate. Raiders were small, organized groups of men with occasional female members attacking wealthy landowners. Their objective was to hit hard and fast, capturing some of the landowner's females and departing with a minimum of destruction. The females were taken to a distant town and then sold to new owners.

Presently, males are the ones in control and power, an ideology born from the "raiding era." Females are now expected to wear collars or restraining devices to show that a male guardian protects them. The collars are designed as jewellery as well as being functional. A female is not required to have a guardian, but under Praxton law, she does not have a lot of legal rights or protection. As far as not wearing a restraining device, and in particular a collar, a woman on Praxton would rather be seen naked. The collar is symbolic of being a woman on Praxton; young girls look forward to being given their first collar and being considered grown up.

Praxton was one of the worlds rebuffing the overtures to join the Alliance worlds and to comply with the Charter of Conduct laws. The world was near the outskirts of human worlds, but did a profitable business in trade with Alliance worlds. Larger than most habitable worlds, Praxton's military style government was secretive about its armed forces, population and wealth. The Charter of Conduct Offices needed more information about Praxton and its decadent culture.

The Charter of Conduct office, first by visiting their tourist zone and then immigrating to the planet, assigned Terri Baxter to spy on Praxton.

She became seduced by the culture on Praxton and the wearing of collar and cuffs. Terri later fell in love with Romie, whom she had accepted as her guardian in order to infiltrate Praxton society. She later resigned from the Charter of Conduct Office.

Chapter One

Terri sat next to Allison on the couch, listening to the newscast on the view screen. Normally, when she was visiting Allison at Master Alex Greggory's home, she had fun laughing with the other five other females as they drank wine and ate snacks. As the night progressed, some of the females often ended up losing their clothes as well. Terri found Allison had a way of not only getting her to lose her clothes, but also managing to join her cuffs together, leaving Terri at her mercy.

Tonight everyone was in a sombre mood as they heard how Alliance forces had launched spacecraft to shut down all transport to and from Praxton and the rest of the galaxy. The only spacecraft to leave were either carrying tourists, or goods purchased loaded on ships belonging to Alliance worlds. Soon all ships would be denied the right to leave or enter Praxton.

The next stage, according to the reports, would be more negotiations between Praxton and Alliance worlds. Unless Praxton was willing to sign the Charter of Conduct, the Alliance Forces would be landing on Praxton to take control of the government. The news reported that for Praxton to sign the Charter of Conduct would likely mean a change in social behaviour on the planet. It might mean the end of the guardian and female relationship currently used on Praxton. Whips, lockable collar and cuffs might also be banned, along with other unique Praxton devices.

So far, the negotiations were not going well. It appeared the Alliance military was going to be setting a deadline for compliance.

Terri and the others went to bed earlier than normal and, as usual, Terri shared a bed with Allison. Terri made herself comfortable earlier in the evening by removing her top and ended up wearing only her skirt. She was used to being undressed in the room with the other females watching the view screen and on more than one occasion ended up nude before going to bed.

Allison, had also on one instance, lightly spanked her in front of the others as she lay naked over her lap, her wrists cuffed behind her back. Terri understood the spanking was a way for Allison to show the others in the room they were intimate with each other. By having Terri cuffed, it showed that Allison was also dominant over her. Praxton females often patted other females on the cheek as a sign of friendship, and a light spanking indicated they were more than friends. It was not necessarily a sign that one was always dominant, though Allison generally tried to get Terri partially undressed and have her wrist cuffs joined together or attached to a short chain when she came over. Terri was usually willing to submit to the younger, smaller but more aggressive female.

Allison was the most junior female under Master Alex, but the others didn't object to her claim over Terri. Allison usually had the fewest visits from Master Alex and generally had to obey the other females in the household. However, Terri was outside the household and had been befriended by Allison, so the senior female Angela thought it was a good opportunity for Allison to express herself sexually.

Terri undressed first and then slid into bed. She watched Allison fold her clothes as she took them off.

"Would you leave your wrist cuffs on, Allison?"

Allison looked at her and then left them on. She climbed into bed and wrapped her arms around Terri.

Terri gave her a hug as they lay on their sides facing each other.

"I'm worried how this is going to end, Allison."

"Me too. Maybe the stupid Charter of Conduct is going to stop females from sleeping together too."

Terri kissed her. "No matter what happens we will be friends, close friends. Understand?"

Allison nodded. "I love you,Terri."

"I love you too." She gave her a long kiss.

Angela, the senior female, walked into the room. "You two okay?"

Terri answered, "Just a little worried, that's all."

Angela went to the foot of the bed and attached a locked cuff and chain to each woman's ankle. She then attached the other end of the chain to the bed. As a senior female, she was responsible for all females under Master Alex, as well as female guests. Traditionally, females were chained to the bed at night, usually with the ankle, but sometimes the wrist or a chain to the collar. Unlike some households, the chains were locked into the place, and Allison and Terri would have to wait for Angela to return in the morning to be released from the bed. For emergencies, a coated key was left within reach. If the emergency key was used, the coating was scraped off as it was inserted into the key hole to show it had been used. Rather than trying to explain why the key was used, most females preferred to call out to the senior female they were in need of assistance. "Try to get some sleep. Tomorrow might be a busy day."

After Angela left, Terri slid down and placed her mouth over Allison's nipple, sucking on it as her tongue licked at it. She paused when she heard Allison moan and went to the other breast. She continued to kiss and suck on Allison's nipples and slowly placed her hand between Allison's legs.

Allison moaned again and spread her legs.

"Good, I got a reaction there. Roll onto your tummy and put your hands behind your back."

Allison rolled over and crossed her wrists.

Terri latched the wrists cuffs together. "Now I have you for a change."

"I guess you do." She looked over at Terri, slightly surprised at her aggressiveness.

Terri played her fingertips over Allison's ass and then squeezed her cheeks. "I want to give you a spanking."

Allison looked over her shoulder at her. "I would like that."

"I know." Terri used her palm to strike Allison's ass, alternating between the cheeks. Each hit was hard and Allison struggled not to cry out.

"Now roll over on your back."

Allison wiggled around until she was on her back, spreading her legs before she was told to do so.

Terri kissed her on her lips and then moved down, laying a carpet of kisses down her neck and to her breasts, where she worked Allison's nipples with her tongue. She continued to kiss and lick at her skin, sliding down over her stomach. She dropped her head between Allison's legs and used her tongue to lick at her pussy.

Allison lifted her hips and cried out as Terri's mouth covered her pussy. She continued to work on her pussy with her hands squeezing Allison's breasts, pinching the engorged nipples. Allison finally cried out one final time and shuddered as her hips fell back to the bed.

"Oh, I do believe I got you good that time."

"You sure did."

Terri held Allison in her arms and hugged her.

"That was very nice, Terri. Why don't you undo my cuffs and I'll do you too?"

"No, I think I'll leave those cuffs joined together tonight."

"Meany..."

"Because I think I'm going to give you another spanking in the morning. I really enjoy paddling you then. There is something to spanking a female when she's under your control."

"Okay, I'd rather you spank me than some other female."

"Slide down a bit."

Allison moved down and Terri pushed her head between her breasts. She positioned a nipple at Allison's lips where she opened her mouth and slowly sucked.

"Hmm, that feels nice. I can sleep like this."

Allison sighed, "Me too."

Terri said thoughtfully, "I wanted you to know tonight that I'll take care of you if things between the Alliance Forces and Praxton get out of hand."

"Thanks." She kissed Terri's breasts. "I feel real good and safe right now."

Chapter Two

Lucinda Taylor felt the shake on her shoulder from her bunkmate. She groaned, wondering why her weekend morning was being disturbed. Unlike weekdays when she had to get up at five forty-five, on weekends she was allowed to sleep in until eight. She glanced at the large clock near the entrance, the readout indicating only ten past seven.

"What's going on?" she croaked out, inwardly cursing the wine she drank last night. She sat up in bed and felt the room swim around her for a moment. "I don't think I can get up."

"Attention, privates! Captain Conley approaching barracks!" Sergeant Colleen MacDonald barked.

That made Taylor jump from the second level bunk she shared with Henley, reaching for her green collar and snapping it into place. Some of the faster privates had managed to pull on a shirt or skirt as they tumbled out of bed. Two came running from the shower, wrapping a towel around them.

Taylor didn't feel she had the precious seconds to pull on something and lined up at the foot of her bed with Henley, who had managed to pull on a pair of panties.

There were four sets of double beds set along a single row. All sixteen females lined up, four of them nude, including Taylor.

Taylor had joined the armed forces as a way of seeing a bit of the world and avoided the need to have a male guardian for a while. The armed forces became her guardian, and she wore the metal green collar to signify that to others. She was a bit taller than the average recruit and did well on the physical training. In fact, the sergeant had indicated only her extracurricular activities might prevent her from getting an early promotion.

That was yesterday, and she celebrated the good review by drinking too much with Marcia Henley and a Corporal Winston. She had seen him around a few times and had notice his stares.

He joined them at their long table, chatting and buying rounds as they laughed at his jokes. He was a big man, and she enjoyed his company, but wasn't prepared to let him get any further that night. Winston, like all males, respected that she wore a collar of another guardian. In this case, it was of the military, but it still meant he was careful not to press his advantage. If they got off military property, or if they were both on leave it might be a different situation, but Lucinda felt secure he would respect her wishes. At most, he could give her a spanking as it was acknowledged males could spank any female if there was a need for it. She didn't give him her first name and didn't ask for his, referring him to him as Corporal Winston at the beginning, and then as Mutton Head, because he confessed his hair was naturally curly and he had to keep it short.

Taylor used her fingers to comb her dark hair and gave Henley's hand a quick squeeze just as Sergeant MacDonald stepped forward.

"Captain Conley, sir!" Sergeant MacDonald called out as she stood at attention. Her uniform was the standard female uniform. A short black and green camouflage skirt, a pair of knee high back boots with a heel, and a form-fitting jacket with a deep V-neck. Her collar was slightly thicker than that of the privates. A minor difference from civilian wear for military women is the use of bras. The military finding going braless in combat might be a disadvantage. Most of the military women went without a bra except during training or combat simulations. MacDonald had large breasts and usually wore a bra to accent them under her jacket. Her breasts, this morning, seem to be straining to get out of the V-neck as she arched her back during her salute.

Captain Conley returned her salute. His uniform was of heavy black and green camouflage pants, dark green shirt, black jacket and heavy boots. He was wearing his combat uniform for a reason and his thick belt held a knife, handgun and rolled up metal chain leash. The leash was a holdover from when the military used to help capture wayward females. Today, it is still a popular military exercise for training purposes.

"I have wonderful news for you, Company G," he growled at them

9

as he walked past them during the inspection. "As you have heard, we will be having our semi-annual chase and capture competition. This year will be different from last year in two respects. One, we will defeat the Green team under Captain Jacob. This is not an option." He looked around the room for emphasis. "The second change will be that we will have female combat soldiers on the chase and capture for the first time." He turned to Sergeant MacDonald.

"Wilkins, O'Neil and Taylor step forward!" She called out their names unnecessarily loud.

Taylor gasped and looked at Henley who gave her a quick grin. She stepped forward and looked at MacDonald who looked back at her standing naked, her hair scattered over her head and looking very much like she was out late last night. She pursed her lips and gave a small shake of her head.

Taylor stood with her hands clasped behind her back as Conley studied her, concentrating on pulling in her stomach and keeping her shoulders back. Of the three females, she was the only one completely nude and felt a bit out of place.

"Soldier you look like a disgrace. I have been up since before five this morning. Even if this is a day to sleep in, you should be able to respond better than this."

"Yes, sir."

"Are you serious about the military?"

"Yes, sir."

He shook his head. "If this wasn't a weekend, I would attach this leash to your collar…" he held up the rolled up chain…"and lead you to the stockade."

"Yes, sir. Sorry, sir."

"Sergeant MacDonald said you would be a good choice for this exercise. Are you trying to make her look foolish?"

"No, sir."

He walked around her and proceeded to the other two females but said nothing to them.

"Okay, sergeant. These will do, on your say so." He glanced at Taylor. "But have Taylor report to me at oh nine hundred. Make that in rough garb."

Taylor took in the congratulations from her barracks and then began to wash up. Rough garb was what military prisoners wore and sometimes soldiers, as well, as punishment. For men, it was only a pair of pants. For females, it was only a very short flared black skirt and a small fitting tank top. It was also the clothing one wore for corporal punishment, and every few weeks some recruit in rough garb was punished publicly in the central area.

Taylor walked barefoot with Henley, who decided to keep her company and defend her from some of the abuse directed towards her. They walked past the mess hall and other barracks along the hard concrete sidewalk. Several other soldiers, male and female, made comments directed at Taylor. She was certain, if Henley wasn't with her, a few would have attempted to pull off her top or skirt. She knew the men just wanted to have another look at a naked female, but the female soldiers' aim was to try to humiliate her even more than she already felt. They reached the administration building, and Henley waited outside the captain's office as Taylor walked inside.

The secretary continued to work on her computer for several seconds before she looked up and acknowledged Taylor. The secretary wore a style of military clothing, composed of a tight fitting jacket held in place by a single brass button, and a tight skirt. The jacket had a wide V-neck, showing plenty of cleavage. The skirt was short, with the waist not reaching the bottom of the jacket. High black boots completed the outfit. Because the secretary, though part of the military, would not take part in military operations, her clothing was designed for show and not practicality. Thus, her boots had a higher heel than the military version, and a bra was not issued. Panties were permitted due to modesty issues for the short fitting skirt. Her collar was military issue, but was of a more elaborate design than most soldiers were.

When the secretary finally did look up, Taylor announced she had appointment with the captain.

The secretary looked her up and down. "We're in a bit of trouble I see."

"Yes, ma'am."

She stood. "I hope you don't make a lot of noise during your punishment. It's hard to concentrate on my work. You're not wearing panties under that skirt are you? That will only get you in more trouble."

"No, ma'am."

"Lift your skirt and let me see."

Taylor lifted the bottom of her skirt to her waist. She knew the secretary was over extending her powers and was just trying to make her feel worse, but there was little she could do. She certainly wasn't going to improve her situation with the captain by getting into an argument with his secretary. She held up her skirt for several seconds, exposing her pussy to the smirking secretary.

"Okay, you can go in now."

Red faced, Taylor was led into office by the secretary and stood at attention as he reviewed her file.

"I should have you spanked or whipped on the central yard you know."

"Yes sir."

"Or would you prefer I spank you here, only this time on your bare ass?"

Taylor swallowed hard, wondering if he was serious. She decided he might well be. "Here sir..."

"Is that because you are embarrassed of what others may think of you and would rather hide your punishment here?"

Taylor nodded slowly, her voiced cracked. "Yes, sir."

He raised his voice, glaring at her as he spoke. "The next time you look like you have been on an all nighter, I will have you spanked naked publicly. I don't give a rat's ass what you do during the night, but you better look combat ready in the morning the next time I see you."

"Yes, sir."

"Do you think the enemy are only going to attack on weekdays? Do you think that we have an agreement with all armed forces that attacks will only occur after breakfast and never on weekends?

"No, sir."

"Perhaps I should check my day-timer for the next enemy attack so I can advise you not to go drinking the night before. Would that be satisfactory to you?"

"No, sir. I mean I understand what I did was wrong."

"How long do you feel you should remain in rough garb, private?

An hour, half a day, the rest of the day to learn your lesson?"

"Sir, I have learned my lesson now, sir."

"Lift up your skirt and bend over the desk."

"Yes, sir." She lifted her skirt at the back and bent over his desk, resting on her forearms.

Conley walked behind her, snapping a riding crop against his pant leg. "Do you think you have learned a lesson today private Taylor?"

"Yes, sir, I have sir."

He nodded, his voice returning to normal. "So you say. Actions speak louder than words. You will stay in rough garb until after lunch. I will keep you on the chase and capture exercise for the time being. Stand up and pull your skirt down. That is all."

She stood up quickly, surprised he hadn't struck her backside. "Yes, sir." She turned and faced him. "Thank you, sir."

A shadow of a smile crossed his lips. "Try to behave yourself in the future."

Taylor left, relieved that was all the punishment she would have to endure. For a moment she felt certain he was going to have her spanked with her leaning over his desk. Still she was going on the exercise and that made her steps a little lighter. Henley walked with her and listened to what happened in the office.

"You were lucky there. He must have taken pity on you."

"I guess so. I just have to make it through lunch now."

Lunch at the canteen seemed to take a long time for Taylor as she sat on the hard bench. She let her skirt flare out behind her and hang over the seat rather than try to sit on the short fabric. Henley kept close to her, the blonde girl acting like her protector from some of the other soldiers who wanted to take advantage of her situation or tease her. She stood right behind Taylor in the food line and told two male soldiers and a female soldier to keep their comments and their hands to themselves. At the table, she ate her own small portion and glared at anyone looking at them.

"Thanks, Marcia." Taylor gave her hand a squeeze as they walked back to their barrack.

"That's okay. I was partly to blame for helping you drink too much last night."

Taylor laughed. "That's right. It was all your fault."

"So you said the old man threatened to spank you and whip you?" Henley grinned, trying to get more details from Taylor.

"Well, he made it sound like he was ready to. He even had me bend over his desk with my skirt raised. I guess it was meant to scare me and it did, though having a spanking might have been better than staying in rough garb until after lunch."

"It could've been both. You look good in that rough garb you know. The men were leering at you and so was Carmen."

"She's always staring at me in the shower."

"Don't worry, I told her you were mine and to keep away."

"Thanks, I think."

"You're welcome." She patted Taylor's bottom quickly. "You know it's not too late for that spanking."

Taylor looked at Henley and gave her a smile, not sure if she was serious. Females on Praxton often had spankings given to them by their guardians. In the military spankings were normally only given by superior officers, but female soldiers sometimes gave a light spanking to each other. In those cases, it was usually the dominant female of the relationship. Taylor knew if she accepted a spanking from Henley, she would be submitting to her as a partner as well. She had thought of herself as being a dominate female before joining the army, at least tougher than the females she knew as friends. But the army, besides the differences in rank, also had a pecking order among females of the same rank. Taylor found that she was among other tough-minded females who wanted to control others.

Praxton society was composed of a higher population of females than males and encouraged the females to develop interest in each other as well as men. The military, when it decided to accept female personnel, also decided to continue the practice of encouraging females to be comfortable with each other. Females in the military slept with another female in a double bed and like most of Praxton female population, they slept nude. Taylor knew Henley, like herself, was interested in men, but also knew there were times during the night they had wrapped their arms around each other, touched each other, and on occasion gave each other a good night kiss. They hadn't had sex yet with each other, but that was partly due to fourteen other people in the room at night. Some of those did not have the same reservations and Taylor sometimes heard the soft moans and sometimes not so quiet cries.

Another part of Praxton society continued by the military was the use of collars for women, and, as a female moved up in rank, her collar became more intricate and wider. The use of spanking and occasionally whips as punishment was common elsewhere on Praxton and though the law forbid permanent skin damage from any punishment, it allowed discretionary use to maintain control. The military extended that punishment to its soldiers as well as imprisonment. Men were usually given imprisonment or the whip. Females were imprisoned, spanked, but rarely whipped. Such punishments may also be done privately or in public in the central area of the camp.

"Relax, I'm just joking."

"You had me worried. I wasn't sure what to believe any more."

"Believe what?"

Both women turned around to the deep voice just behind them.

Taylor replied, "Hi there, Winston."

He was grinning at them and she was sure he had seen Henley pat her ass.

"Never mind..."

"Hey, Taylor, I heard you got selected for the big competition. Congratulations."

"Thanks. I'm pretty excited about it."

"You should be. First females selected."

"Yeah, I know."

"Guess what? I'm also on the chase and capture competition. We're going to be on the same team."

Taylor looked at him. "And that's a good thing?"

"Watch it or I'll have you over my knee before you can say rough garb."

"Right..." Taylor stretched out the word and was pretty certain he was just joking, grinning back at him.

He walked with them to their barracks, joking with them and telling Taylor he was looking forward to working with her on the chase and capture exercise, giving her a wink in the process.

After he left, Henley elbowed Taylor "He seems pretty interested in you. Last night and today he walks you back to the barracks."

"Walked both of us."

"Walked you. He's cute, and you're going to spend some time with him on the chase and capture exercise."

"I don't know if he's my type."

"Oh come on, if he's not your type, who is?" Henley challenged her.

"Okay, he will do."

"What made you join the military anyway?"

"I came from a real small town, Bristol. When I came of age, I looked at my options. I could continue to live at home, but I wanted to see more of the world. Bristol only had a few possible guardians, and I didn't really feel they were who I was looking for. I could put myself in an auction, but that's a bit risky. I know government regulations make them safe, but I could end up with a guardian I don't like. I was thinking about putting an ad out for a guardian when I came across an article about letting the military be your guardian. I looked into it and thought it would work for me."

"You didn't want to go the freelancer route?"

"No way. That's not for me. I want a guardian. How about you? Why did you join the military?"

"I wanted to leave my guardian. I wasn't sure what kind of guardian I wanted next so I decided the military would give me time to think about it."

* * * *

Nicole Adams puffed as she ran up the slope of red sand and gravel interspersed with small yellow plants, her feet slipping as she tried to make headway. Her hands reached out to prevent herself from falling when she stumbled at the top of the small hill.

Panting, she crouched down and surveyed the landscape, looking for signs of the Red Team and the rest of her pursuers.

Nicole was twenty-six and in the best shape of her life. She was tall at just one inch under six feet, but slim. She critically assessed her own figure as average. She had slim hips, small waist with average sized breasts. Men gave her figure a higher rating than herself, often making positive remarks on her black, long hair.

She tossed back her hair and prepared to sprint along the rifts between the rolling hills. It was hot, and she stopped to take another drink from her canteen before starting to jog again, dodging around small boulders. A plant with brittle branches snagged at her leggings, making her curse quietly under her breath. The leggings, like her top, were made of a stretchable green, red and yellow camouflage material. The material was breathable, but had a couple of drawbacks. It was skin-tight and once it tore in one spot the tear would spread. So far, Nicole had managed to tear only a few spots, mostly on her pants.

Nicole guessed she had to last at least another hour to give herself and her team a chance to win.

The rules were simple. Two sets of three female fugitives were given a twenty-minute head start at a point twenty kilometres from the main base. Each of the female groups was placed in the opposite direction of the base camp. Individually, and as a team, they were to try to either avoid capture as long as possible or reach the main base. Trying to capture each group was a military team made up of ten members.

All the fugitives were volunteer freelancer females, carefully chosen to make sure capture was not going to be easy. All six females received five thousand crowns to start, with an additional ten thousand crowns to each of the winning team. In addition, the one with longest time before capture received another five thousand crowns. In the unlikely event a fugitive made it to the home base, there was a bonus of ten thousand crowns.

The two military teams were not given a monetary reward to capture their fugitives first, but did so out of pride. The winning company received special recognition, a one-week leave and the right to display a trophy in the mess hall. Those who were selected for the hunt usually were being watched closely for a possible promotion as an added incentive.

Each fugitive had the same type of clothing and kit consisting of water, a first aid package and a transmitter one could activate if they became injured.

The money was the sole reason Nicole entered her name into the tournament. She arrived on Praxton just over two years ago to make money and to have an adventure on one of the few worlds that had rejected the Charter of Conduct. Praxton wasn't considered a safe world by Alliance world's standards.

The money was proving to be lucrative and she enjoyed the different relationships she received as a freelancer. After a time she was able to adjust to the paternal, chauvinistic society, though her earlier visions of finding a man to settle down with faded as she gave up on a string of relationships.

She had agreed to a personal services contract for her first year on Praxton, bored with living on Treator and the planet's quiet resort like conditions.

The first year was the most difficult, signing a contract that allowed her employer complete control over her as a guardian. She had made a provision in the contract that she would not have not endure public humiliation, nor absorb punishment through whips or other devices causing pain. Her employer wasted little time before he did want he wanted, ignoring anything in the contract not in his favour.

Nicole had a choice of leaving Praxton immediately without payment or staying under protest. She didn't mind some aspects of being under his control, the sex was good and she quickly got use to the collar and other restraints. The whips were a different matter. Her owner didn't push her limits, but being spanked in front of others was humiliating at first. At the end of the year, she almost stayed with him and his two other females, but decided there was more money to make elsewhere.

At first, it wasn't easy, but she was now making considerable money and would be able to leave Praxton a wealthy woman in a few years. Her choice to become a freelancer meant she gave up protection of a guardian, and the law rarely provided any protection to a female being taken advantage of by a male or another female. Nicole relied on her quick wits and martial arts training she took on Treator to keep out of trouble. It wasn't always successful. Freelancers were treated with contempt by other females and males looked at her as someone to capture for their own uses. But many men were willing to pay her well for the pleasure of her company for a short period of time, sometimes for hours and occasionally for a week.

Nicole made her way quickly between the hills, heading south towards the home base. She knew it was rare for anyone to make it there, but not entirely impossible. The military personal pursuing her consisted of seven male and three female soldiers. In this exercise the soldiers were not allowed the use of electronic sniffers or other devices to help seek her out, giving her a mild advantage. The soldiers, however, were well trained for the topography and knew how to pick up tracks of the fugitives. She knew it was impossible for them not to pick up some of her tracks eventually, but she hoped to delay how long it took to find where she was going. A full out sprint was unlikely to work as the soldiers were well conditioned to run continuously. Thus, she was going to have to be devious to elude them. It would be a difficult task. The reward for the soldiers was not monetary, but pride in winning over the other team and bragging rights. That would make them even more determined to find her.

* * * *

Lieutenant Lloyd Gallagher crouched on one knee and inspected the ground carefully as his team milled about. He stood after a short time and surveyed the land around him.

"Okay, listen up. One of them has headed towards the flats. Judging by the footprints, she's probably running. Johnson, Mason and Persani, you three go after her. If her trail goes away from the flats, radio us, but I think she's just trying to make up distance. Go."

"Yes sir." The three sprinted off, two of them looking identical, except for a slight difference in height. The two men were wearing the loose fitting grey and red camouflage fatigues and tall black boots. They also wore gloves, yellow goggles and a cap. Johnson wore the female version of fatigues. That consisted of high boots, tight camouflage pants and matching top.

He waited until they left and resumed speaking. "The other two have headed towards the hills. Once we pick up the trail there, we'll divide up. In the meantime, let's make time."

The rest followed him as he jogged towards the distant hills.

Gallagher led a quick pace, confident the rest would keep up easily. He was honoured when the captain chose him to lead the team. Unfortunately, he wasn't given the privilege of picking out the other members; that was done by the general himself who was known to pick people to test the capabilities of the team leader.

It was yet another accolade for Gallagher who had additional barriers to join the military because he wasn't born on Praxton, arriving when he was twelve when his parents immigrated to the planet. His parents were geologists, and though his sister hated living in the small isolated town, Robert fell in love with the desert like landscape that covered much of the world. When his parents and sister left seven years later, he decided to stay on his adopted home.

Chapter Three

Nicole kicked at the lizard rat that scurried by her foot. The native, foot long creature looked like an Earth lizard, but with a thin, rat-like tail. They were harmless, but she didn't like being startled. She took another small drink of water and continued to circle back towards her pursuers. She knew they had their methods of tracking her and hoped she could trick them by moving in a circle. Nicole was pleased she had been able to maintain a high pace despite the strong sun, knowing her head start would disappear soon.

She completed the circle and then made a leap to a flat rock. She stood on one foot and brushed the loose dirt away from her to obliterate her footprint. Then she leaped again, this time on loose dirt. She tried standing on her toes as she brushed away the dirt underneath her before taking another jump and starting to run through the terrain again.

Nicole didn't think much of the camouflage suit when she was given it in the morning. Like most women's clothing on Praxton, it was designed to show off the female figure. In this case, the thin material clung like a second skin, not hiding any part of her form. As with some of the other fugitives, she decided not to bother with underwear, knowing regardless how the hunt went, she was likely to end up naked at some time during the festivities. That didn't matter; the monetary rewards did.

Nicole now was running as fast as she dared on the uncertain terrain, trying to increase the distance from her to the pursuers. After about ten minutes, she made a sharp turn to the east towards the plains. She guessed the plains were an obvious choice for the inexperienced and that anyone trying to use them for the home base would be quickly captured. The hills allowed more opportunity to hide and delay capture. However, she guessed that not many would suspect someone would change from the hills to the plain and thus she might remain undetected longer. Coupled with her circular trek, she hoped to have confused the military.

* * * *

"Lieutenant Gallagher, sir!" the radio barked out, breaking his concentration of the ground as he looked for disturbances.

"Go ahead."

"Sir, we have spotted fugitive one and she has detected our pursuit. She has made evasive action towards the hill. Position approximately fifteen hundred meters from base line zero, sir."

"Continue pursuit. I'll send reinforcements to cut her off."

"Yes sir."

Gallagher turned to Winston, a six foot three well tanned male. Winston had a minor weight problem, but was shedding pounds as his military career continued.

"You and Taylor are to intercept fugitive one. Position yourself at fifteen hundred meters from the baseline and one hundred meters east of base row. Report when you have made the capture."

Gallagher now had five personnel after the first fugitive and hoped the capture could be made quickly, as he wanted as many people as possible to cover the hills. He rejected sending Winston by himself. Rule number one was to always use at least pairs in tracking. The second choice was Taylor, a dark haired female who kept her locks under her cap. Because this was an outdoor assignment, she was allowed to switch from her normal short skirt to a pair of tight fitting pants. Like the men, the women had tall black boots, but hers were fitted and actually had a small heel. Her top was a stretch fit as well and her outfit, while camouflaged like the men's, was meant for show and not for practicality. Not many women joined the military service on Praxton, knowing that it was difficult to gain promotion in the male dominated organization.

* * * *

Winston led Taylor over a couple of small hills. Soon they were out of sight of the main group.

"Come on, Taylor, you're slowing me down." He grinned at her as she pushed herself up the slope. She looked up at him and shook her head.

"Yeah, well try running in these boots Mutton Head."

"Hey, a little respect..." He smacked her on her ass as she caught up to him.

"As if..."

He patted her bum a couple of more times, not hard, but enough for her to turn around and wag a finger at him.

"Hey, we're supposed to be catching a fugitive." She turned and sprinted towards the next hill.

"We are. But sometimes the troops need a little encouragement now and then." A moment later, he caught up to her and again patted her ass as he stepped by her.

They continued to run and jog. Winston took additional opportunities to grab at her. Occasionally Taylor would slap at his hand, but otherwise ignored him. They had known each other for the past few months, but it was only during Taylor's recent celebration she spent time with him. Fraternization on the campground was discouraged, but when an opportunity of leave or in this case, field training occurred, the soldiers tried to take advantage of it.

"Okay, this is the position where Gallagher told us to wait. Let's hide behind this rock." He pointed at a sandstone rock slab that stood six feet above the ground. One side was flat, while the other side was a normal shaped rounded rock. They pressed against the flat surface, and moments later Taylor felt his hand on her ass again.

"Hey, Taylor, are you wearing panties?"

She turned to look at him. "None of your business, Mutton Head."

He leaned into her and circled his hand along her waist, slipping his fingers inside the waistband. "I figure you must be wearing real heavy ones to slow you down so much."

"Trust me, they're not heavy." She tried to pull his fingers away, but he reached to her front with his other hand and in a quick, jerking motion loosened her belt. She switched her hands to her loose belt but by then he also succeeded in undoing the top snap of her pants. She gripped the waist of her pants, thinking he was going to try to tug them down, but instead slipped his hand alongside her left hip.

"Winston! Not here for crying out loud." He continued to lean against her on the flat surface of the rock and she felt his stiff cock press against her backside.

With a sudden pull, he snapped the elastic waistband of her thong. Then his other hand moved to her right hip and again she felt the snap of the elastic waist.

"Hey those were perfectly good army panties." She twisted her head back to look at him.

"Were." He reached inside the front of her pants, grasped her panties and slowly began to pull them out.

"Winston, that's not fair." She gasped at the sensation of the ruined panties sliding between her legs and she looked down to watch the black thong come out of her pants. He then held the panties high above his head, whirled them a couple of times and then stuffed them in his trouser pocket.

"Didn't you get one on your panties raid two months ago?" She tried to glare at him but suspected her own flushed expression was giving her emotions away.

"Hands above your head, soldier." He pressed at her right elbow to lift it up.

Taylor wasn't sure if she had much of an option as he outranked her. That also meant if they got caught, he would be the one held responsible. She raised her left hand to grasp her right, intertwining her fingers on top of her head.

Winston tugged her shirt up and over her bra. He unhooked the back strap and then took his knife and cut the two shoulder straps. He stepped back as he sheathed his knife.

Taylor stayed flush on the stone wall, not moving her hands even though her pants had slipped down to her lower hips, exposing the top of her cheeks.

"About face soldier. Keep your hands above your head."

She turned around slowly, keeping hands above her head and watched as he reached out to pull away her ruined bra. The black bra was stuffed into his pocket as well.

"Very nice, Taylor." He surveyed her medium sized breasts with large dark nipples. He reached over to her pants and undid the remaining fastener. Her pants were tight fitting and slid only a few more inches, but the open fly exposed her stomach almost to her groin. "You shave completely?"

"Obviously."

He took his time to stare at her bare skin. "I guess you do, Taylor."

"Call me Lucinda, since this is getting rather personal." She did a quick check at her own breasts, noting her nipples were engorged and erect. She also saw the bulge in his pants and decided that maybe they should wait. "Look, that girl is going to be coming here soon and if we're caught with our pants down, there'll be hell to pay. Let's hold off until the party tonight, we'll have a chance then." Pausing briefly, she asked, "what's your first name?"

He considered her words as his right hand pushed his erection to a more comfortable spot. "Eric. Damn, I suppose you're right. Okay, let's watch out for the female."

Taylor breathed a sigh of relief, pulled down her top and fastened her pants again. She saw her nipples were leaving an impression under the shirt, making it obvious her bra had been removed. Praxton military didn't require her to wear a bra, so she wasn't going to get in trouble for it. Praxton military was one of the few places on Praxton where women wore bras, and she was used to not wearing one and more comfortable without it. The military also was the only place where females didn't always wear a dress or skirt. The first time Lucinda put on pants she found covering up her legs odd. She did like how the tight pants showed off her ass, but that was the only thing she liked about them.

Fifteen minutes later, they heard the noise of someone scrambling over the hills. A blonde woman was panting as she looked behind her, unaware of their presence.

"Go get her, Lucinda."

Taylor was pleased. Usually males wanted all the glory, but she had just been given a chance to make the first corral of the fugitives. She realized that Winston probably just wanted to watch two females wrestle, but she still wanted to prove she could use her training to subdue the fugitive. She ran hard at the blonde female, who was bigger than she was in both height and weight. She also had larger breasts, perhaps one of the reasons she was chosen as one of the fugitives.

The blonde didn't see her until it was almost too late. Taylor hit her from the side, and the two rolled down the slope. The blonde recovered quickly and tried to push off her off. As they wrestled on the ground, Winston came running up, but stopped short of interfering.

The blonde groped at her shoulders as Taylor sat on her stomach. It was close to an even match, but the blonde was already tired from her exertions running along the hills. Taylor ignored her hands, clutched at the fabric of her top and yanked. The result was as she expected, the cloth tearing open to expose the blonde's breasts. It was as they had taught her in the military classrooms. When attempting to subdue an opponent, if you have an opportunity to make them feel exposed whether by removing armour or clothing, doing so will usually weaken resistance. Taylor and several of the others then had that demonstrated to them on a first hand basis. Psychologically, it was a powerful weapon.

The blonde woman opened her mouth in astonishment. She stopped pushing against Taylor, and after the fabric was completely ripped open at her front, tried to cover her breasts with her hands. Taylor took hold of her long blonde hair as she began to stand up.

"Roll over, bitch, and put your hands behind your back."

As the blonde complied, Winston reached into his backpack and tossed over cuffs, collar and a length of chain. Within a minute, she had her hands cuffed behind her back, and a length of chain attached her wrists to the back of her collar. When the collar and cuffs locked, a circuit was closed that sent a signal to the command post that the fugitive was captured. The signal also verified the time and the identity of the female when the capture was made.

Winston radioed in. "This is Winston. We have secured Fugitive One. Would you like us to bring her to you or to home base, sir?"

There was moment of time before Gallagher replied; no doubt considering whether he should send two of his personnel to escort the fugitive back. Policy indicated using at least two soldiers to escort single prisoners, or to have the fugitive with them that could slow down their pursuit of the others.

"Return the fugitive to home base."

"Sir."

Winston looked pleased. "We got the first capture and we get to lead her back to the base!"

Taylor grinned. "That's great!" She turned to the blonde. "What's your name?"

"Sophie."

"Okay, Sophie, you're our prisoner now. Let's not have any more resistance."

The blonde didn't look as pleased as she rolled to sit on her knees. The cuffs on her wrists were wide, black hard plastic with an inner rubber sleeve that expanded to prevent the wrists from slipping out. The rigid cuffs forced her arms to be stacked one above the other, and movement was further restricted by the short chain to her collar. The collar was made of the same hard, wide plastic material, but wasn't tight.

They began to trek west where a service road ran towards the base. There they would meet up with a military jeep to carry their prisoner to the home base.

Winston looked at the blonde and noticed Taylor was observing him. "Nice tits on her."

"I was thinking afterwards that you probably enjoyed it when I ripped open her top."

"Hell, I was hoping you'd strip her completely."

"I'll bet you were."

He paused for a few seconds. "You know it's not too late."

"I don't know. What's it to me if she's stripped?" Taylor thought Winston was horny enough without seeing a naked female. Besides, she didn't need the competition for his attention.

"Tell you what. We strip her, attach a leash or something, and you can lead her into the camp."

"That sounds interesting."

"Wanna do it?"

Sophie followed the conversation. She knew protesting wouldn't do a thing to help her, and just might encourage them to attach a gag. The one thing she was glad of was the company of the female soldier. Female military officers were generally known to be crueller than their male counter parts when it came to female prisoners, but in this case being alone with a male while being in restraints, didn't appeal to her. Being stripped naked and in cuffs was going to be a humbling experience, but she had been prepared for such an eventuality when she agreed to the military exercise.

Taylor looked over at Sophie for a few seconds. "Okay, Blondie, I guess you're going to lose the rest of your clothes."

Taylor, using her fingers and her knife, removed the rest of her top. Then she made a small tear with her knife on the pants and ripped the fabric off. Sophie closed her eyes and grimaced during her ordeal.

She stood there wearing a pale yellow thong.

"Hand me those panties, but don't tear them. Take off her boots too. Make her go barefoot."

Taylor bent down and undid the boots, pulling them off. Then she reached up, pulled off the panties and tossed them to him.

He took them and shoved them in his pocket.

"Getting quite a collection of female underwear there, Eric. Satisfied now?"

"She's looking better all the time."

"Yeah, from a guy's standpoint I suppose." She handed him the remains of the shirt, pants. "Here, stuff these in your backpack or your pocket. We can't leave anything lying around or there'll be shit later on." She reached into her own backpack and pulled out a length of blue rope.

Sophie complained. "Please. I'm not resisting. Do we really need to attach that rope?"

Taylor hesitated for a second, and then continued to pass the loose end of the rope through a metal ring in the collar. "I won't pull it tight, unless you make me. But you must know this is standard for prisoners. Or would you prefer a crotch rope that is sometimes used on female prisoners?"

"No."

"Then be thankful you were only stripped." She turned towards Winston. "Enjoy the show, Eric?"

"Oh, yeah..."

"Why don't you just jerk off then you pervert?" She grinned at him as he stared. The bulge in his trousers had returned. She talked quietly to Sophie who was looking anxious at being naked and in restraints.

"Don't worry. He's not going to do anything. And I won't tug on this rope if you behave. Understand?"

Sophie tried to nod but the collar restricted her movement. "Okay."

"Okay, Mutton Head, we're ready to march."

They walked towards the service road, with Sophie stepping carefully on the sand and pebble surface. A dark blue, jeep like vehicle with an extended rear deck that could seat six approached. In the front sat two soldiers dressed in dark green uniforms, a male driver and a female medic. Both stepped out of the vehicle at their approach. The male wore the traditional military uniform, while the female's medic uniform consisted of a short skirt that covered only a foot below her hip. A jacket, with a deep V-neck, that didn't quite reach the top of her skirt, completed her uniform besides the high heeled shoes. A white armband indicated she was part of medical team.

Winston spoke first. "We have a fugitive available for transport back to the base."

The driver and the medic grinned, though the medic approached Sophie.

"Are you okay physically?"

"I'm fine."

The five climbed into the jeep, though Sophie had to be assisted as she sat next to Taylor.

"What's going to happen to me now?"

Taylor shrugged. "You and the other fugitives will be paraded, maybe with minor discipline, in front of the troops. It's mostly show, though there might be a bit of discomfort. Then there will be a party that you get to attend. Just get used to being naked."

"Great. I can hardly wait." Sophie added sarcastically.

Chapter Four

Diane Fulton took the shuttle to the closest shopping mall, deciding to spend her last day shopping. The mall looked like many of the malls back home, but with a few differences. All of the Alliance world's chain stores were missing and replaced by store names she had never heard of before. The Charter of Conduct Office, in their efforts to produce a homogenous society, encouraged the development of multi-world chain stores. The Charter of Conduct Office believed if the same products and clothing were common throughout the various worlds, there would be less difference between people and therefore more harmony.

A second difference was that almost all the shoppers were women. That was due at least in part to the much higher population of women to men on Praxton. But females on Praxton were expected to dress and be prepared for each day more so than any other world. Therefore, they spent time looking for the right clothes, accessories and makeup.

Diane browsed in the various shops, feeling conspicuous and nervous. She saw that many of the females were wearing an elaborate combination of collars and cuffs linked by chains. Usually the chains did not restrict them too much, though the occasional female was partially hampered in their movements. In those cases, it was usually a chain between the ankle cuffs that prevented full steps or chains that didn't allow full reach of their arms. These females were being escorted by another female that carried a leash in her hand, usually folded and not attached to the collar.

Diane knew her own collar was simplistic in design compared to the others and her cuffs looked plain without the chains attached to them. She also noticed the other women wore more revealing clothes. Besides the shorter skirts, their tops often showed off the breast and nipple jewellery. She received curious, but not hostile looks from the other shoppers and she tried to keep her composure as she window shopped. She finally went into a shoe store and the saleswoman gave her a warm smile.

"You look like you're new to Praxton. Are you an immigrant?"

"No, I work for the Alliance government. I'm here on business." Diane didn't want to admit she was part of the Charter of Conduct Office, the organization that was known for trying to convert Praxton society to more of the Alliance ideal. "I really like the shoes women wear here and would like to bring back a couple of pairs home."

"Of course." She pointed to the shoes on display. "As you have noticed Praxton shoes have a much higher heel than most worlds. The sides are usually cut away to show off more of the foot and the back of the shoe can have an intricate fastening; usually long straps that wrap around the ankle."

"They look hard to walk in."

"You do have to get used to them, but Praxton shoes are not just for looks. They have an excellent arch support and are not tight fitting at the toes. You will find our shoes do not pinch, so you can wear them for extended periods of time. The important thing is to find a pair that fits properly, don't worry about the shoe size. Wear what fits you comfortably."

Diane purchased three pairs and then asked where a good store to look at collars was located. "I'm curious on the different types, not that I'd wear any back home."

"Of course, but you may find the collars work as jewellery on Alliance worlds. I understand it's a new fashion trend on those worlds. Try Trends Collars, just up one floor."

Diane walked into Trends Collars, taken aback by the number of display cases and the size of the store. She walked slowly by the collars, chains and cuffs displayed. She was surprised at the number of different collar styles shown, including wide, narrow, hard metal, soft fabric, plain, and jewel encrusted.

It appeared the sales staff was content to let her browse by herself for a few minutes before approaching her. Eventually, a lady slightly older than herself greeted her as Diane stared at a silver coloured metal collar.

"Can you tell me something about that collar?"

The sales lady smiled. "Certainly. You have a lovely accent. Where are you from?"

"I'm originally from Tobar, but now work for the Alliance government. I'm here on business." Diane didn't think her accent was all that different from those on Praxton, but obviously it stood out well enough to indicate she was from off world.

"I hope you're enjoying your time here. That collar, like all the collars in this display case come as a set. That means, besides the collar, there are matching wrist and ankle cuffs. A set of chains are also included so that that the cuffs and collar can be joined. The collar and cuffs are all hinged and are held closed by a magnet and a lock." She took out the collar and opened it, revealing small hinges that were hidden when it was closed. "All collars in this selection use a built in lock. Once the collar is closed, one presses this small button and the collar is locked. The key is inserted to unlock it here." She indicated a small hole below the button.

Diane examined the collar, turning it carefully in her fingers. "You don't have to lock it though do you? The magnet will keep it closed?"

"The magnet will keep it closed, but is meant just to align the locking mechanism. Collars are meant to be locked. You see, the collar is a symbol of a female's relationship to her guardian. If it's not locked, it implies she can take it off any time she wants, that he has no control over her." She took out two keys from a drawer. "These are the keys that go with the collar. They are identical, except this one is covered with a hard wax. The male keeps the spare key to unlock the collar. This other key the female keeps, but she may not use it except in emergencies. He will know if she unlocks the collar or cuffs, because the wax will be scraped off the key to use it."

"Oh, so she needs his permission to remove the collar."

"True, though a senior female will also have permission to use the key. In practice, the female is often given a duplicate key to remove it in her bedroom, to change or to wash up. Females should never leave their bedroom without a collar on."

Diane felt the smooth metal of the cuff and slipped it over wrist, looking at the effect. "I see, but I don't have a guardian, so there wouldn't be any need to lock it."

"But you would know. You feel different knowing your collar and cuffs were locked and the key wasn't in your possession. I suggest locking the collar and leaving the key at home." She looked at Diane's collar. "I thought that since you are wearing a collar you had a temporary guardian."

"I guess in a way I do have a temporary guardian." She decided not to explain that Troy LeBlanc was pretending to be her guardian during her time on Praxton. "What is that collar? It comes with a belt?" She pointed inside the display case. The two-inch wide belt was made of metal hinges every inch along the length. A small metal ring was located between each hinge.

"That is a lockable belt. The belt is usually tight fitting and the rings along it are meant to hold chains. The chains are then attached to cuffs. It is designed to restrict movement of the female as much as possible, while still allowing her to move around. Sometimes a chain is run from the front of the belt to the back and between her legs. The middle of the chain is often fitted with a small oval ball and sits between her lips."

Diane pulled a face. "That seems rather harsh."

"No, not really. It's a source of stimulation." She held up the belt. "Isn't it pretty? And the collar and cuffs have a nice cut on the metal surface."

Diane touched the belt. "It doesn't feel rough at all."

"You must try it on." She walked around the counter and wrapped it around Diane's waist. "You can adjust how tight you want it by sliding the clasp at the side here. We won't make it too tight."

Diane heard a small click as the belt was locked. "Well it's not uncomfortable."

"It complements almost any outfit. A full set of chains of different lengths are included so your guardian can decide how much freedom you may have."

Diane decided not to correct her again on not having a guardian. She was also toying with the thought in her mind that he was her guardian that he could keep her collared at his pleasure. She looked at the belt and felt it press against her stomach.

The saleswoman slowly placed one of the cuffs on Diane's wrist and then joined a short chain from the belt to the cuff. "It looks very nice with the chain to the cuffs."

Diane nodded, breathing deeply as she watched the saleswoman place the second wrist cuff on her and attach the chain as well. She tried to move her hands about, finding she was just able to reach one hand to the wrist of the other. "Not much freedom there."

"No, but different lengths of chain can be used. Shall I get a set for you or do you want to try the collar on first?"

Diane walked out of the store with the belt and its set of cuffs, chains and collar. She also took a second set of collar and cuffs made of a yellow metal. She wondered what she would tell anyone if they found that she, an official from the Charter of Conduct Office, was buying collars and cuffs.

Her next stop was at a clothing store where she purchased some of the see-through tops the woman on Praxton liked to wear and some of the short skirts. The tops, she figured, could be worn under a jacket without causing a problem on Alliance worlds and the short skirts would be acceptable as casual wear when she was not at work.

Diane was excited about her purchases as she walked down the mall. She had her own set of collar and cuffs to wear, along with the revealing fashions. She was feeling aroused at the prospect of putting on her new items behind the closed door of her suite. As she headed towards the exit, she made a sudden decision to go into a small jewellery store.

There wasn't a big demand for necklaces or other jewellery sold on Alliance worlds as collars and cuffs took over as accessories for necks and wrists. But with the high visibility of breasts, other adornments became popular. Breast jewellery and temporary tattoos were popular, as well as, nipple jewellery. Diane was amazed at the number of designs and styles available.

The saleswoman explained the various types to her.

"Some of these just sit around the nipple and make it more prominent under the top. There are different designs such as plain rings, stars, butterflies or geometric figures. Some of them have small loops to which you attach a chain. You can join the nipple clips together with a single chain or use a pair of chains and attach them to the collar."

Diane examined a clip carefully. "Do they hurt?"

"No, not at all. You just press them into place. There's another type that has adjustment in them, like a clamp. Sometimes your guardian will tighten up those and will cause a temporary discomfort."

"Well I just want to look at ones for cosmetic reasons."

"These are nice." She pointed at a small display on the counter. "Once in place, they push your nipple forward, making them easy to see under your top. These all come with a small chain to run between the nipple clips. Looks really nice if you're topless or wearing an open shirt." She opened her own shirt to reveal a glistening chain between her breasts.

Diane considered she had already bought a lot of the unique Praxton fashions and might as well go all the way. She purchased three pairs of nipple jewellery and then her phone began to chirp.

"Hello, Diane Fulton speaking."

"Diane, this is Ambassador LeBlanc calling. An emergency situation has just occurred, and you must return to the embassy in all due haste."

"Yes, ambassador, I understand."

Diane used her phone to call for the embassy's shuttle. She felt anxious as the shuttle landed at the embassy.

Diane Fulton hurried inside the front doors. She was the Charter of Conduct Office representative assigned to go to Praxton with the purpose of bringing the former spy, Terri Baxter, back to Earth and be retrained. Her mission had failed, and worse, she realised that she found the unique Praxton fashions interesting enough to go shopping to bring several items home.

The receptionist was standing just inside the entrance, looking nervous.

"Ambassador LeBlanc is having an emergency meeting in the main boardroom on the second level. We have to hurry, they're waiting for you." The receptionist pressed a button on the desk to switch incoming calls to an electronic answering system. "Follow me please."

Diane followed her at a fast walk, for a female, to the elevator. Praxton females were taught to walk slowly and with a gentle hip swing. Diane had copied their walk, in part, because she also wore the high-heeled shoes Praxton females used that forced a careful step. A minute later, the doors opened up and the receptionist led the way to the boardroom. As soon as they walked in the room, Troy LeBlanc stood up and gestured for them to sit down. Diane found a chair at the end of the table and sat down, trying to hide the shopping bags from the other dozen people in the room. She carefully placed the bags on the floor, hoping the collar, cuffs and chains would not spill out. Diane was intrigued by the short skirts, the revealing tops and the high-heeled sandals, but was even more excited to try on the nipple jewellery and restraints. That would now have to wait until she had some privacy.

"I will be as brief as possible," Ambassador LeBlanc spoke in a clear voice that carried the weight of authority behind it, "and I will try to answer any questions you may have afterwards. However, be aware I have limited information myself, and we don't have much time for speculation.

"The Alliance worlds have given an ultimatum to Praxton. Accept the Charter of Conduct as law or there will be military consequences. Protocol dictates that the embassy should be safe from any military action and I don't believe Praxton will make us a target. However, there is always a danger from inadvertent strikes, and I must inform you of that possibility. In the event of the embassy being struck, the fire alarm will sound, and I will ask everyone to move to the basement of the building. I suggest everyone keep a small bag with some personal essentials, and ensure that sensitive data is not far from your person. Currently, only tourists are allowed to leave Praxton, and we have been advised that until further notice, embassy personnel will be treated as spies if we leave the compound."

Diane listened to LeBlanc's speech and the hurried questions afterwards, her thoughts on how soon she might be able to leave Praxton with her purchases. After the meeting, she rushed to her room to repack her suitcases with her new clothes, jewellery and restraints, pushing them under her other clothes. She then made up a small bag of what LeBlanc called personal items. She looked at the suitcase that held her Praxton items and took a deep breath to calm herself. She already had come up with a cover story if anyone discovered what she had bought on Praxton. She was going to indicate it was only souvenirs, as she didn't expect

Praxton to continue as an independent world. Still in the back recesses of her mind she longed to put on the collar and cuffs and see how the nipple jewellery looked and felt.

She decided to talk to LeBlanc to see if he knew how long she was going to stay in the embassy. She knew the ambassador knew more than he had revealed at the meeting, but hoped he would give an indication when she might be able to leave. She knocked on his office door and entered when he called out.

LeBlanc smiled warmly as Diane explained to him that technically she wasn't embassy staff and therefore shouldn't be treated as a potential spy.

"Unfortunately, the Praxton government is not very discerning in that regard. You are part of the Alliance government and therefore are a potential spy. As far as the timetable when you might leave, that is hard to be certain of. First, the Praxton government has three days to comply with the ultimatum and second, if hostilities do break out, it might be several days for the Alliance forces to secure the cities." He continued to look caring and friendly as he spoke.

"So I'm looking at over a week here?"

He nodded. "Possibly longer."

Diane crossed her arms and frowned.

"I would suggest you try to make the best of the situation. Your suite is quite comfortable and nicely appointed. The embassy is not large, but we do have an excellent cooking staff and other amenities."

"But you also indicated that we may be attacked..."

He raised his hand. "Inadvertently."

"Alright, inadvertently, but still attacked. We would then have to live in the basement."

LeBlanc smiled with his teeth showing. "I would suggest that is not a likely event. True, the embassy may be hit by stray fire, but I suggested the basement only as a temporary refuge. I misstated the gravity of the situation slightly during the meeting to make sure everyone was prepared and aware of what they had to do. Still the basement is not a harsh environment and we will be comfortable there on a short term basis."

Her hands dropped to her sides and her frown lessened.

"I do have a suggestion for you. I recommend you send out any information you need to send to the Alliance government as soon as possible. I would not be surprised if all communication outside of Praxton is suspended during the conflict."

"Okay, I will do that immediately."

"Good. If you should like, I would be pleased to give you a tour of the basement so you can see for yourself the facilities are quite pleasant."

She was surprised at the friendliness in his voice, and decided he was trying to make up for their earlier arguments when she first arrived on Praxton. He had insisted that she wear a collar and the Praxton female fashions if she was going to do work outside the embassy, explaining it was her own safety and in the interests of maintaining relations with Praxton. She had resisted his demands and argued with him. In the end, she had to comply with his wishes and wore a collar that indicated to those on Praxton she had a male guardian. She had found, as time went on, that she enjoyed the Praxton fashions and didn't find the collar uncomfortable.

"That would be acceptable. I would like to be prepared if the need arises that I have to go down there." She also thought there was a developing chemistry between them. His company might make her stay more enjoyable.

* * * *

The basement was not as she expected. She thought it would be more of a storage area, but it seemed to be more of an entertainment area for visitors. There were two small meeting rooms and an office that the ambassador indicated was for his use. But there was also a large ballroom with a well-equipped bar and a kitchen located next to it. She noticed there were several other rooms down a hallway, and one more entrance to the basement she didn't expect to see; next to the ballroom, large patio style doors opened to a grassed area with trees and flower beds.

As he gave her a tour she took a brief look through the doors and saw a brick wall surrounded the enclosure and realized the garden and the ballroom was used to entertain political guests. It appeared the garden area was dug out and the brick walls were used, at least partially, to act as retaining walls. Diane scanned the area and saw two eight high foot posts on either side of the patio doors that looked a bit out of place in the manicured garden.

"What are those posts for?"

"I will give you the long explanation. As ambassador, I represent the Alliance government and try keep misunderstandings and conflicts to a minimum between us and the Praxton government. To that end, I often have social engagements here where I can show the positives of being part of the Alliance worlds. Some of these benefits are best explained over glasses of Alliance produced wine. To make the visitors feel comfortable, I also observe some of the Praxton customs, customs of which you have indicated you disapprove.

"However, for me to ask them to consider joining the Alliance worlds, I must show a willingness to observe their culture and beliefs. I do this by making this lower floor a place where Praxton culture is observed, while bending their ear to the benefits of the Alliance worlds and the Charter of Conduct."

"So they feel at home here and therefore more likely to listen to your arguments?"

"Not arguments, suggestions. But you are essentially correct."

"And the posts...?"

"On Praxton, once a year, they observe a day called Reconciliation. It is basically recognizing a time in their in history when their civil war ended. Reconciliation day is not so much a celebration, but a time when a household invites friends and neighbours to come over for dinner and social interaction. A big part of Reconciliation Day is the offering of females to the guests. Traditionally, one or more females are left outside the front entrance as a gift to the visitor and as a peace offering. This has evolved to females being bound with rope outside the front door at most homes. Usually, such a female is nude and great lengths of rope or other material are used to tie her in a pose that is supposed to be artistically pleasing while not being too uncomfortable."

"So women are being offered as gifts? Incredible."

"No, that part of the tradition no longer applies. The females are just for display only. It is considered an honour for the female to be chosen to represent the household, by the way."

"So those posts are used to display females during this

Reconciliation Day?"

"Yes, we usually ask one of Praxton officials to supply us with two females for the event. They consider it a compliment that we ask them for this favour."

Diane looked at the posts and tried to picture two naked, bound females being used to greet visitors to embassy. For an instant, she pictured herself tied naked to a post, having been ordered by the ambassador to be displayed for the arriving guests. Her hands were secured above her head and rope wrapped her body tightly to the post as visitors stopped to view her.

"Ms. Fulton?"

Diane jumped back to reality. She hoped he didn't suspect her thoughts and her now suddenly erect nipples weren't visible under the pale yellow blouse. "A very barbaric custom," she spoke quietly.

"Perhaps, but the custom was born out of peace, and that is something we need right now. Allow me to show you more of the facilities."

She nodded and tried to follow him a half step behind so that he couldn't observe her nipples, and perhaps guess her reaction to the information about Reconciliation day.

He pointed at two doors on his left. "Washrooms, both with shower facilities."

"That's good to know. Are there any areas for sleeping?"

"Yes there are, but perhaps not what you have in mind." He turned towards a double set of doors, opened them to a large room and stopped to allow Diane to enter first. "You may wish to take off your shoes. The floor is made up of an open weave carpet and you will find the heel of your shoe sinking in. The floor is designed to encourage the female to be barefoot."

She took in the rectangular room and removed her shoes, dropping them by the doorway. She was puzzled why they would want women to be barefoot in the room. She began to walk towards one end of the room where she saw a row of steel chrome bars, finding the floor spongy under her foot. "Are those prison cells?"

"No, they are cages, specifically designed for females."

She turned to look at him in amazement, but then continued her journey towards them. The five cages covered one end of the room and were about six feet deep by four feet wide. The top of the cages didn't quite reach the ceiling and used the same chrome steel bars to cover the top. Along one side was a narrow bed that was hinged lengthwise so it could be folded against the cage bars. The cage was otherwise empty, save for hooks mounted at intervals on the bars.

"What is the purpose of these cages?" Diane placed her hand around a shiny steel bar and swung open the door.

"As I indicated, we try to follow the Praxton social customs and it is expected that homes and places of social interaction there will be a place to keep females. Why don't you take a look inside?"

Diane stepped inside the cage and walked along the short length, her fingers touching each bar as she went by. She reached up and found she could just reach the top of the cage bars and noted some hooks to hold restraints attached to one of the bars. Her heart was beating fast as she turned around to face LeBlanc. She suddenly felt vulnerable. He was standing holding the cage door with one hand as if he was prepared to close it on her. Diane became intensely aware of her collar, her revealing clothes and being barefoot. Without the height of her shoes, he looked bigger and powerful as he stood there smiling slightly at her.

"What do you think about being inside the cage?"

Diane was aware his question was directed not only as asking her opinion about females being put in cages, but also a subtle hint about her being locked inside the cage. He was blocking the only exit out of the cage and he could quickly close it on her. She knew how she should answer the question, with anger and disgust on treating women that way. But she also knew her voice would betray her and her answer would lack conviction. Instead, she asked, "How long were females kept in cages like this?"

"Not too long, normally, perhaps a few hours, but sometimes a day or two." He swung the cage door back and forth a few inches casually. "Of course, if you were to be kept in here, you would normally be nude, except for your collar of course." .

Diane nodded and swallowed.

"Restraints are sometimes used in the cage as well."

She tried to control her breathing and relax. It seemed likely he was

41

only teasing her because of the way she first acted when she arrived on Praxton. But there was a second problem. She could feel her nipples becoming engorged as he spoke of having her naked inside the cage. She was becoming aroused and she was positive he was using key words on her and watching her reaction, reminding her of the collar she wore. She watched the cage door slowly inch towards being closed. "That is all very interesting." Her voice came out quietly and she could no longer meet his eyes.

"Would you like to see what it looks like with the door fully closed?" He slowly inched the door closed without waiting for her answer.

Diane watched the chrome bars come together. Her mouth opened to say something, but only silence came out. Then she heard the click as the lock engaged and she closed her eyes for a moment. She walked slowly to the cage door and pushed against the bars, testing their strength. Diane leaned on the bars and closed her eyes, feeling the cool steel on her cheeks. Her breasts were pressed between the bars and she knew LeBlanc could see them outlined perfectly against the blouse's fabric.

"Most females do not necessarily see being in the cage as a punishment, though sometimes it is used as a form of discipline." He spoke quietly, standing only a few inches away from her on the other side of the cage door.

"I understand. Are you going to open the door now?" She opened her eyes and looked up at him.

"Do you really want me to unlock the door? Perhaps I should keep you in here so you will be out of harm's way."

"Keeping me safe? What would be next, restraints?" She tried to give a hint of sarcasm in her voice and realized she hadn't answered his first question, if she wanted him to unlock the door. She wanted to absorb the feeling of being locked in a cage for a few more seconds and stepped away from the door to do a small circle inside the cage, taking in the bars around her. She heard a click and knew he had unlocked the door.

"Perhaps I will have another opportunity to demonstrate the cage to you."

She declined to reply, just meeting his eyes for a moment before stepping slowly past him and outside the cage. She didn't trust herself to speak, wondering if she could muster the strength in her voice that showed him she was not a push over. She feared he knew she was completely flustered.

She studied another wall opposite of the cages containing hooks spaced at intervals to hold restraints in place and the high benches that appeared to have the sole purpose of holding a female in a secure position. A box held an assortment of whips and restraints. "Females are punished in this room with these whips?"

"Yes. On Praxton it is expected that females are occasionally disciplined. Not harshly, but to maintain order in society, it has to be done. For example, a female will be tied naked to these benches and be lightly whipped. The whipping is done in such a way as not to damage the skin and only stings a bit. Of course, the discipline is also sometimes done in public so the female also feels some humiliation as well."

Diane recalled the Black Steel video where she had watched a nude Terri Baxter being whipped with a coloured foam whip that left glowing paint on her. She had found the whipping erotic...arousing. She supposed part of the appeal was the crowd shouting in the background, knowing that her naked body and the punishment were seen by everyone. The public humiliation made it even more exciting. She was wondering why LeBlanc was showing her this room in such detail and speculated it was more than to just prepare her in case the basement had to be used.

"Do you disapprove?"

Diane pivoted slightly so he couldn't see her face. Standing in her bare feet close to him definitely was giving him an advantage and she believed he was able to read people's faces easily, no doubt a big advantage as an ambassador. "I think I've expressed my feelings about Praxton society when I first arrived here."

"You did at that. But have you changed your opinion in any degree since you've been here?"

"Perhaps, but that is normal after one has a chance to spend time around the population."

"Then returning to my original question, do you still disapprove of Praxton culture?"

"It is what it is. My approval or disapproval doesn't make any difference."

He chuckled softly. "You have the makings of a fine diplomat with your answers. Come. Let me show you the kitchen." He gently enclosed two fingers just above her elbow and turned her towards the door.

Diane was aware of the careful way he touched her. In Alliance worlds, there were some cultures where it was considered impolite to touch anyone unless they were in a social setting. Other groups were comfortable with a lot of touching and standing in close proximity. The Charter of Conduct solution was three quarters of an arm length away from another individual and touching could be done only with a hand between the shoulder and the elbow. While the regulations were not normally enforced, it was expected that government employees and officials always practice them. LeBlanc followed the protocol perfectly, but by enclosing his fingers around her elbow, he managed to state he was in control. She didn't resist his push at her elbow, knowing she was admitting his dominance.

At the doorway, he diverted her to the opposite side where she left her shoes and he bent down to pick them up and carried them a few steps before offering them to her. Diane took them, but noticed he wasn't stopping to allow her to put them back on. She knew he was indicating he wanted her to remain barefoot and she wondered if she should challenge him by stopping to put them on.

He gave her another of his full-fledged grins. "Come, my secretary must be wondering where I am."

She nodded and continued to carry her shoes, knowing he had cleverly fabricated a case where time was running short. If she did stop to put on her shoes, and the sandals required the weaving of a long length of lace around her ankle, it would look like she wasn't concerned about his time.

LeBlanc opened the kitchen door. "As you can see the kitchen is fully stocked and has the facilities to prepare a banquet, if needed. If we are forced to stay down here, any of the staff is free to use the kitchen to make meals."

Diane stared at the stainless steel appliances. "At least we won't go hungry."

"No, we won't." He pointed towards a second door in the kitchen,

"And this leads back to the ballroom." He led the way. "Often we have the room filled with tables and the catering staff use this door to serve the meals."

The ballroom was empty, save for a few long tables set against a wall. She considered there was a reason why he took her to the ballroom and walked slowly around, looking at the decorations on the wall and ceiling. Some were paintings and photos from Alliance worlds and others were obviously from Praxton. The ones from Praxton were either of the landscape of the reddish soil or of naked females held in restraints. He was waiting for her to ask a question and she doubted it was to comment on the pictures. She turned towards the tables and walked towards them. They looked solid, and then she noticed attachments at the corners and the middle of the table. "These tables look different."

"The tables are used during cocktail parties and less formal engagements, where we don't have the full meals. Instead, we set up snack tables with hors d'oeuvre, but with a difference."

She didn't wait for him to continue. "Let me guess. It has something to do with females." Diane crossed her arms, but failed to come up with the stern look she was hoping for.

"That is true. We have nude females lie on the table, in restraints of course, and use them as platters for food."

"You put food on them?"

"Yes. Occasionally a dip is put on their breasts, cheese and crackers on their stomach or perhaps chocolate on their thighs."

Diane studied the tables. "That's very interesting. At least it would save on dishes."

He laughed at her joke. "You don't act surprised."

"Nothing would surprise me about what they do to women on this planet."

He gave a small chuckle. "Perhaps you will be here long enough to enjoy a party here where you can experience the Praxton culture."

"Enjoy would not necessarily be the word I would use."

They walked back to the elevator slowly, and Diane turned her head back once more to look at the tables. "It would be uncomfortable being on the table all night in restraints."

"It wouldn't be all night, perhaps a couple of hours. I don't believe they mind too much. You can try it if you wish." He chuckled at her sudden blush.

"I hardly think so." Diane wished she could put more force into her words. They sounded hollow to her own ears.

The elevator doors closed behind them.

"Would you be averse to joining me in the lounge for a few minutes? I would like to discuss some business with you pertaining to our present situation between the Alliance world and Praxton."

"I guess I can do that." Diane wondered why he wanted to discuss the situation in the lounge rather than in private, but assumed he wanted a less formal setting knowing she was feeling apprehensive.

Once again, he gently guided her at the top of her elbow as they exited out of the elevator and towards the lounge. Diane decided not to react to his subtle control over her until she heard what he had to say in the lounge.

The waitress brought them a decanter of red wine to share and LeBlanc began his discussion. "As you may well have guessed, I wanted to show you the basement not just to show the facilities, but also to describe some more of how Praxton views society. This is not an evil world. The crime rate is exceptionally low compared to Alliance worlds and most of the citizens do not wish to leave here to live on any of the Alliance worlds."

"I have noted that already."

He nodded, "Then perhaps you have also noted the female population likes the way things are here, that they accept what you described as barbaric behaviour?"

Diane took a drink of her wine and avoided looking at him, feeling chastised for using the term barbaric earlier. She slowly returned the glass to the table and spoke quietly. "Perhaps barbaric wasn't a good word to use." Then to herself, *And yes the women here accept this control men have on them.*

"There is a conflict between the Alliance worlds and Praxton. I ask you to extend what influence you have to halt any military action against this world. I want you to tell those who will listen, that you do not believe the population, male or female, want the Charter of Conduct imposed upon them. Will you do this now that you understand Praxton better?"

"I don't know and I'm not sure what influence I do have in such matters."

"Everyone has some influence, and do you really wish to take away Praxton's freedom and how the people want to live, even if you don't agree with it?"

She slowly nodded. "I see your point of view. While I don't condone how females are treated here, I suppose to a degree it is their choice, and the Charter of Conduct shouldn't be forced on them all at once. I will send in a report expressing the view that the proposition be done over an extended period of time."

"Thank you. I believe that freedom of choice on how a planet wants to live is something, that as an ambassador, I have an obligation to understand, to help work towards peace. The Charter of Conduct is a goal we have to strive for all planets, whether they are part of the Alliance worlds or not. To accomplish that, sometimes we have to show we appreciate their society and then gradually get them to implement the Charter of Conduct."

"I have to say it certainly has been an eye opener that people and society can be so different from the Alliance worlds."

"And the Charter of Conduct...?" He smirked and refilled both their glasses. "Tell me, have you been conscious of the collar you are wearing?"

Diane reached up and touched her collar with her fingertips, lingering at the metal ring at the front. "I guess I stopped noticing I was wearing it, but I'm aware of it."

"Do you understand that it is not just a symbol of a female being under the control and protection of a guardian, but it is also a piece of jewellery?"

"Jewellery...? I suppose it can be seen as an elaborate necklace."

"Believe me, some of these collars can be quite expensive in their design and can include gems. The one I gave you is somewhat simplistic in style, but some are made out of metal with an artistic pattern. May I make a suggestion?"

"Of course."

"Try to emulate Praxton fashions while you are here. It may help you understand their way of thinking. The collar is in many ways a fashion statement. I suggest you complement it by adding matching wrist cuffs. I think the cuffs on a sleeveless top will be quite attractive on you. It doesn't mean you are submitting to a guardian, just that it gives you a balanced look."

She took another drink from her glass and was beginning to feel a slight effect from the potent Praxton wine. She thought of her own purchases safely hidden in her suitcase; the metal collar with matching wrist and ankle cuffs that came with a set of silver chains. "Perhaps you are right, that I should try the Praxton fashions if I'm going to make a report on it."

"Excellent. I will have Carol Miller bring you a matching set to your suite. I'm sure you'll find it interesting to try on. More wine?"

* * * *

Diane Fulton opened the door to Carol Miller who was holding a small package.

Diane felt a bit giddy as Carol explained the ambassador asked her to bring her jewellery pieces to wear.

"Oh thank you. I'll try them on later."

"Well actually, if you don't mind, he instructed me to put them on you, and have you join him for dinner. There will be another couple as well."

"Oh, dinner...? Well I suppose so. Is it a formal affair? Do I need to dress up?"

"I can help you pick out something and get ready. I have brought some makeup for you to try as well."

"Alright." She showed Carol her clothes hanging in the closet. "I brought some formal wear with me when I packed."

"They look nice, but perhaps I can get one of the dresses the embassy keeps in a storeroom. They are more of the Praxton style and will go better the collar and cuffs." Carol felt the fabric of a couple of the dresses. "Why don't you get undressed and I'll help you with the makeup?"

Diane sat still, wearing only a thong, as Carol showed her how to apply makeup to her breasts, dusting her skin with a small brush. The brush tickled her skin as she watched how Carol accentuated the curves and smoothed out the skin using a small amount of powder. A black dress lay on the bed, borrowed from the embassy's storeroom. The sheer top of the dress necessitated the makeup on breasts and later the nipple jewellery, which Carol also had to show her on how to put on.

"There, I think that looks really good. Let's put on the dress and the rest of the stuff."

"Thank you for helping me with the makeup. I've never had to worry about putting makeup on there before." Diane slipped the dress on and looked in the mirror, pleased with what she saw. The sleeveless dress was opaque at the bottom, but became increasingly transparent at the top, where it ended under her arms. "The jewellery is quite light. I hardly feel them on."

"They look really nice on you." She held up a white metal collar with three metal rings attached to it. "Let's put this on now."

Diane watched her encircle her neck with the collar and latch it into place in the viewscreen that acted like a mirror. A second later, she saw Carol close a small padlock on the collar. "Is that really necessary?"

"Oh, yes, it completes the look. The collar just doesn't look like a collar without the lock." She continued as she put the matching wrist cuffs on Diane, "I know how you feel. I remember the first time I put on a collar and it was locked. It was a very special moment for me." Carol added two more padlocks and then bent down to attached ankle cuffs.

"Was that with Gordon, the guy who wants to be your guardian?"

"Yeah, I'm in love with him but… it's still a big step."

After locking the ankle cuffs Carol stood and attached a silver chain from the collar to each wrist cuff. "These chains won't reduce your arm movement too much, but they add a bit of contrast to the black dress."

Diane nodded and put on her shoes. The shoes had a higher heel than she was used to and she spent a few seconds adjusting her balance. "This Gordon fellow. You said you're in love with him?"

"Yes."

"I was in love many years ago. He was, is, a wonderful man. But I turned down his proposal because the Charter of Conduct Office wanted me work on a different planet than where he was stationed. I figured I'd forget him and find another man easily enough." She looked in the viewscreen one more time and then turned back to Carol. "If you want my advice, follow your heart. I wished I had."

They walked together down the hall to the private dining room.

"Thanks for the advice."

"You're welcome. Don't I need a key to undo the collar and cuffs later?"

"The ambassador said to give the key to him. It's normal for the guardian to hold the main key."

"Okay, what about a second key?"

"He wants both of them, although he did say to ask you first."

Diane shook her head. "He is a bit devious, isn't he? Sure, he can keep the keys for the time being."

"He's also unattached. Have a good time." Carol giggled and left Diane at the doorway to the dining room.

Chapter Five

Nicole hid behind the rock outcropping as she observed the blonde fugitive wrestle with the female soldier. It was a close call. She was heading east when she heard running footsteps and dove to hide behind the rocks, eventually raising her head to see who was causing the noise.

The fugitive was bigger and stronger than the soldier, but was shy on technique. She almost escaped the grasp of the soldier, but was tripped up and after another short wrestling match, found herself pinned down. When her shirt became ripped, she gave up resistance.

The male soldier only watched and seemed to enjoy the struggles of the two females. That was fine with Nicole. The longer the first fugitive was free of the restraints, the longer the clock ran. The overall time of all three fugitives was added up and a minute could make the difference between winning and losing.

Nicole didn't move until the fugitive was put in restraints and then led away. She then sprinted towards the plains again. The flat area was a poor place to begin an escape. It was easy to track the fugitive and there were few places to hide. But now Nicole figured that the military wouldn't suspect that someone would go there afterwards and wouldn't be looking there. Regardless, she was going to use the flat ground only to make up some distance for a short time before returning to the hills. If she could keep them guessing where she was going, she had a better chance of staying free. Most fugitives headed in the north-south direction to attempt to reach the base camp. The last few kilometres to the base were an open area, and she thought it was unlikely anyone could make it. At that point, trying to sprint and outrun well-conditioned soldiers wasn't feasible. But Nicole just wanted to extend her freedom as long as possible and get the smaller, but still substantial bonus award. That meant instead of trying to reach the base camp, she was going to run around in circles in a random pattern. That might confuse her captors enough for her to win.

The sun was making its presence felt as the day progressed. While the morning was cool when she started out, it was now warm and within the next few hours, it could get hot. Nicole made sure she took regular sips from her canteen and was now glad the material she wore was breathable and helped keep her cool.

Voices! Nicole froze in her tracks and slowly crouched down, trying to determine the direction of the sound. It was a male voice that had to be talking on a radio, as only his side of the conversation could be heard easily.

"Yes, sir. There isn't any sign of any other footprints." Pause.

"Understood sir. Mason out."

"What does he want us to do?" A second voice spoke, also male but deeper.

"He thinks one of the fugitives was doubling back, trying to confuse the trail. So he wants us to go back to the plains, and see if there might be a second set of footprints."

"Well, maybe we'll get lucky this time. We almost had that first fugitive, but she spotted us too soon." The third voice spoke, this one female with an accent.

Nicole waited until their footsteps disappeared, then slowly continued her way east. If they were heading the same direction as her, she decided it would be safer to follow them to the plains. At least this way she knew where they were. It was a dangerous game to trail them, the prey stalking the hunters, but at least now, she now wasn't just moving about randomly.

* * * *

Lieutenant Gallagher let the sandy dirt trickle from his fingers. The first fugitive had been easy to catch. He had a fix on the direction of the second fugitive and that would be his next priority. She was heading over the hills north of the home base in a straight forward, deliberate pattern. She was making good time, but he was certain they could capture her within an hour.

But the third fugitive was giving him pause to consider. She had circled back and then had carefully continued her northward direction. After some confusion, he had picked up her trail again. But now she was moving east. Before she had circled back again and traveled north for a short time. The trail was getting obscure in a few places, and when he tried guessing where her next place was, he found nothing. That meant a time consuming search of the area until he could find the trail again. "She's a tricky one."

"Sir...?"

"Nothing Bradford, just musing to myself." He stood up. "Miller and McKean, you stay with me. Bradford you take the others and go after fugitive number two. Her trail is straight forward."

"Yes sir!" He snapped a salute, looking pleased he was going to lead the rest.

"One thing. There's a medic on the transport jeep and she's checking if there are any physical injuries to the fugitives, no doubt because of that incident last year. So when you apprehend her, do not use excessive force and do not molest the fugitive. You can strip her, but that is as far as it goes or my ass will be in a sling and yours will be doubly so."

"Sir."

"Now go."

"Yes, sir." Bradford signalled for the others to follow him and took off at a fast pace.

* * * *

Nicole continued her silent trailing of the soldiers. She decided she would follow them for another fifteen minutes and then break off in a different direction. "No point in pressing my luck," she mumbled to herself.

Gallagher studied the map and tried to figure out where fugitive three was going. It was obvious she had a plan and not just running. While most fugitives tried to get to the home base, she appeared to want to just evade capture as long as possible. What was even more maddening, he wasn't sure where she was right now, only where she was two hours ago on the speculation of smudged footprints. He looked at the horizon. *If I was her, and only wanted to avoid capture what would I do? I would circle around to confuse the trail and then move off in a direction no one would think I would do. Okay lady, I know what your game is now.*

* * * *

Yvonne grimaced. Her right arm had blood trickling down below the elbow and her right knee felt badly bruised after tumbling down a small embankment. She had laid on the rocky soil for five minutes clutching her knee before gingerly getting back up and limping along again. She was pleased she had lasted this long, but knew the heat was sapping her strength now. The shaded areas were still cool and she hugged the hills as she looked behind her. No one was visible yet, and she paused for another drink of water.

She continued her steady progress towards the home base and then spotted a figure slightly ahead of her and to her right. She stopped and turned to her left, crouching behind a large boulder. A voice called out to her, making her jump.

"Stay where you are. We can see you."

She stood up, looking around. A female soldier stepped out into the opening between the boulder and the next set of hills. Yvonne paused wondering if she should run back where she came or try to get around the soldier.

"Don't even think it. Try to escape now and I'll kick your ass. Want to be dragged back to camp naked? Then drop to your knees or else that'll happen." The female soldier was now only a few yards away, approaching her slowly but with confidence. Yvonne's knee was still sore and she knew she wasn't going to outrun or outfight the soldier.

"Okay, I give up. But my knee is banged up, I can't bend it."

Johnson didn't look impressed by the confession. "Whatever. Turn around and put your hands behind your back."

She complied and felt the plastic snap around her wrists and then the collar around her neck as two male soldiers stepped into the small clearing as well.

One of them spoke into a radio.

Gallagher listened to Bradford and then replied, "Good work. You and Johnson escort her back to the main camp using the transport. Make sure you inform them that the fugitive had an injured knee from before the capture. Tell Connick to make his way back here. If he spots the third fugitive, he is not to try to apprehend her, but to radio us immediately." Gallagher decided to follow the proper protocol of avoiding having one soldier try to capture a fugitive by himself, even though he was sure there wouldn't be problem there.

"Let's go McKean, Miller. McKean, you take the left rear, Miller the right rear position.

Forty-five minutes later, they met up with Johnson, Mason and Persani.

"Damn it! Didn't it occur to you to look behind you occasionally?" Gallagher looked at the fourth set of prints. "She was following you, you and you!" He pointed a finger at each one of the soldiers. He glared at them. "Okay, we're going to fan out. This time think as you look."

Gallagher was angry with his soldiers, but was also reluctantly giving the last fugitive more and more credit on her ability to confuse them.

"Miller, come with me. Bradford, lead the others along this route." He opened a map and showed him the area he wanted him to cover.

"Yes sir. What direction are you heading?"

"I have a hunch she's going along here, along the plains."

"But she's been hiding pretty good sir, and that's right out in the open."

"So we wouldn't think of looking there normally would we?"

Gallagher led a quick pace with Miller puffing as she tried to keep up. He reached the plains that skirted the jagged rocks and hills and studied the ground as he stepped up his pace even more. Miller began to jog to keep up to his long stride.

"Look Miller, fresh prints!"

"Excellent sir, should we inform the others?"

"Yes, tell them we're closing in on her along the west point of the hills."

Miller began to speak into the radio when she saw the blur of the fugitive leap on Gallagher's back, causing him to tumble to the ground. She rolled back up quickly and kicked hard at the back of his right knee.

Miller ran over to assist him, but the fugitive deflected her attempt to grab her, punched her in the stomach and then tripped her on Gallagher as he tried to get up.

Nicole knew it was a calculated gamble. They were closing in on her fast now, pinching in on her from two sides. She was surprised that two of them had figured she was using the plains now and that eliminated her best chance to get to home base undetected. Unlike the females on Praxton, she had taken an aggression course on fighting, not the usual defensive courses. She noticed he was traveling with a lone female and decided to risk a surprise attack. If she could disable him, she thought that would give her considerable lead-time to get away. The female, she wasn't as worried about if she came to his rescue. The trick was to render him unable to pursue her without leaving a permanent injury, that may lead to her being disqualified from the money. A soft tissue injury would work, if she could surprise him.

Gallagher stood up with Miller's help and radioed Bradford.

"No, I think she will go back into the hills. Have Mason and Persani watch the plains to be safe, but I think I know where she's going now."

Gallagher hobbled towards the hills again.

"Sir, don't you think I should call a medic for you?"

He glared at her, his voice quiet but filled with determination. "Don't you fucking dare. I'm going to capture the bitch that jumped me. This is personal." He turned his back on her, limping faster as he hurried.

Nicole ducked inside a small cave as two soldiers went by. She held her breath, wondering if they would recognize the dark shadow as a cave. A few minutes later, she crawled out and made her way carefully among the hills, getting more confident that she was getting by the last soldiers. She crawled on her stomach over another rise with the red rock tearing at her clothes and her skin. Later she came across an embankment that was too steep to walk and half-slid—half crawled down the slope.

She followed the gully for a while and climbed up a series of shale like rocks to reach the top of another hill. She looked around carefully first and then slowly stood up. She brushed the loose pebbles from her front, noticing most of the fabric was torn and there were a dozen scratches on her chest and stomach. Her legs were mostly bare and blood seeped out of several scratches. She took a drink of water and carried on, climbing down the other side of the hill.

She walked along a narrowing path between two steep slopes when she confronted a female soldier. She considered taking her on, but she might have backup close by and she was getting a little tired from climbing over the rocks. She turned around quickly and saw him standing not six feet away.

"This time you're not getting the jump on me."

She looked down at his knee. "I may not need it this time." She leaned into her stance.

She tried a series of kicks that he blocked and then retreated. Then he counter attacked with a fury under which she wilted. Nicole went down to one knee with her hands raised. She saw his closed fist, the arm ready to strike the blow. She closed her eyes and rolled away. She sat on the ground and looked back up at him.

"You have a choice. Kneel in front of me and let me put on this collar and cuffs or get up and try to fight me." His eyes had a no nonsense look to them.

She got up slowly, feeling the bruise on her ribs, and formed her stance again.

Once again, they fought, but this time the battle was short as she ended up on her back on the hard ground. Her top was almost completely torn off now and she stared at him as he stood above her. She knew one of her breasts was exposed and suspected he had a nice look at the erect nipple. She slowly rose again, facing him in an uncertain stance.

He stepped towards her, his arm swinging across to knock her down again despite her attempted block. She rolled and slid on her backside feeling the fabric rip into tatters; her bare cheeks scraped by the rough ground.

"Get up, or kneel in front of me."

Nicole heard the anger in his voice, felt the ache in her body and knew she couldn't stand again as she gasped for air. She glared at him.

"Are you too weak to even kneel in front of me?" he challenged her.

She struggled to her knees, feeling angry and aroused at the same time. Nicole crawled on her knees the two steps to be in front of him, her arms hanging by her sides.

Gallagher latched the black collar on her neck and then roughly cuffed her wrists behind her back. Then, in a sudden jerk, he tore away the rest of her top. He stared at her heaving breasts.

"Satisfied now? You made me kneel in front of you. A warrior's victory, I suppose."

He frowned at her and helped her to her feet by pulling up at her arm. Her words rang true to him. He did feel very satisfied in his victory. He looked at her torn pants.

She saw where his eyes went. "Does the great warrior plan on stripping me completely?"

"I still might."

He looked over at Miller to tell her to radio that Fugitive three was officially captured. She was looking at him as well, though more at the region below his waist. He looked down at the bulge in his pants and turned away from her as he spoke, slightly confused. "Radio her in Miller, that is, radio we have made the final capture."

He hooked a leash to her collar and began to lead her out of the hills.

Miller trailed behind the fugitive, having to hurry to keep up, but not willing to risk the wrath of her superior and ask him to slow down. Miller hoped the fugitive didn't fall down. That would cause possible problems if she got injured in their custody. But she noticed something was going on between the fugitive and Gallagher. She looked flushed and not just from the heat. Gallagher had a reputation of a serious, procedure-driven Lieutenant. She was somewhat shocked to see an erection under his pants when he had subdued the fugitive. She half expected to see that happen on some men, but Gallagher? This, she decided, had the makings of some great gossip.

Nicole found his pace too fast as he limped on ahead. He occasionally tugged on the chain leash attached to her collar if she slowed down at all. "Please, not so fast. It's not my fault I surprised you. I was supposed to try to get away."

A few steps later, he slowed and stopped, slowly turning around.

"You're right. I was pissed off that you surprised me." He looked at her, taking in her bare breasts and going back to her worried face. "Are you alright?" His voice softened.

"I hurt all over, but yeah, I'm okay."

"Sorry if I was too rough on you." He turned towards Miller. "Clean her up some. Put something on her scratches and wipe her face."

Nicole closed her eyes for a moment as Miller wiped her face clean with a wet cloth from the first aid kit.

"Is he always so moody?"

"No, can't say he is. I heard he pushes hard. He was born off world so he has to work harder to get promoted. You jumping him made him a little upset, and I guess he had to prove how tough he is."

"He's plenty tough. Does he have to stare at me like that? I'm not going to try to get away."

Miller looked over her shoulder at Gallagher as he leaned on a rock. He was watching them intently. "I think he likes you actually. I heard that he doesn't like weak women, so I guess he finds you interesting. There, you look better now."

"Thanks."

* * * *

The rumours Nicole heard that they forced the fugitives forced to stay nude while put on display in front of the troops, were unfounded. They were given new clothes to wear and were invited to both the dinner and the party afterwards. Nicole wasn't surprised when Gallagher approached her after the dinner. "I'd offer to buy you a drink if they weren't already for free."

She grinned. "You could still walk me over to the bar and get me a drink."

He walked with her to the bar. "So now what are going to do? You won the big prize of being the last capture."

"My body aches all over. I think I'll make an appointment for a body massage and take some time off. Do you get any time off after this exercise?"

He passed her a drink from the bar and gently placed a hand at her back to lead her away from the crowd. "Yeah, I get a week."

"What are you going to do with it?"

"I hope to find a pretty companion to spend time with."

Nicole blushed at the intensity of his gaze, but didn't look away.

Gallagher slowly reached over and placed a hand on her waist. "I wish we could have met under better circumstances."

"You mean you didn't enjoy ripping off my top?" Her lips parted as he drew closer.

"No, I'm talking about you kicking me in the knee."

She laughed. "I was a poor female just trying to escape."

"Well, see if you can escape this." He pulled her close and kissed her.

She returned his kiss, closing her eyes and wrapping her arms around his shoulders.

After the kiss was over, she kept her arms around his neck. "I wish we could've met under different conditions as well."

"We can still get together. Have you always been a freelancer?"

"No, had a guardian first when I came over here."

"Ever consider having a guardian again?"

She shook her head. "No, I need my freedom and my own finances. You can't do that with a guardian." She remembered the high reward she received for being the last fugitive captured.

"True enough. But I think we could get along rather well, providing you don't jump me from behind again." He grinned at her.

"Don't let your guard down with me around then. Yeah, I guess we would get along rather well." She grinned at him, thinking how strong he looked in his dress uniform and remembering how she felt when he ordered her to kneel in front of him.

"Too bad you won't let me be your guardian. I think my collar on you would look rather nice."

She lowered her eyes and felt a blush coming on. "I may not want a guardian, but I didn't say I wouldn't wear your collar."

He was silent for several seconds. "Then in that case may I get you another drink?"

* * * *

Lucinda Taylor took her drink outside with Winston. Eric led her around another building far away from the mess hall where the celebration was being held and began to kiss her.

"Did you leave off your bra as ordered private?"

She returned his kiss, murmuring, "Yes, sir."

"And panties?"

"None, sir."

"Inspection time, we need you out of uniform for that." He removed her top and then undid her skirt, pushing it down to the ground. He kissed her neck as he cupped her breasts.

She moaned as he kissed her, his lips going down to her breasts and then sucking on her nipples. His hand reached down between her legs and he slowly inserted a finger inside her.

"Lucinda, you're still wearing your boots."

"I'm still not out of uniform?"

He dropped to his knees and began to unfasten the black high boots. "We need you completely naked."

"Have I been bad, sir?" She watched him pull off her boots and toss them to the side. "Are you going to punish me?"

"I think I should. Perhaps a small paddling is in order."

"Yes, sir." Lucinda turned around, leaned against the building and pushed her backside away a bit. "Perhaps you should cuff me too."

She crossed her wrists behind her. She heard him fumble with the wrist cuffs and secure her wrists. "Don't make the spanking loud. Someone might hear." Lucinda figured that was enough of a hint that she wanted him to be her guardian. Instead of a collar, she figured the cuffs would make him appear in charge with the spanking to show she was submissive. She hoped being naked and under his control would lead him to wanting to collar her later.

"Then let's go farther away." He led her past another set of buildings. "I want to spank you good."

"You do, do you? Well I guess you can do what you want, I'm pretty much helpless."

He smacked her ass several times.

"Ouch! I think that's enough of that."

"No, not yet." He spanked her again, several times, then looked down at her. "Now I think your ass is nice and red.

"I'm very sure it is. Now are you going to make use of that cock of yours or just leave me frustrated?"

"I'm trying to decide on a blow job or your pussy."

"I'll give you a blow job later. Satisfy me first."

He chuckled as she began to lie down on her back on the grass. As he undid his pants, a siren began to wail.

"Oh shit! What is that?" She rolled to her knees and began to stand.

A loudspeaker announced, "This is not a drill. Report to the staging area immediately. This is not a drill. Report to the staging area immediately. All personnel, report now to the staging area."

"Oh, double shit." Lucinda got up. "Everyone is going to think I line up naked all the time. Unlock my cuffs quick."

Eric complied, but then took off running, leaving Lucinda standing naked.

Lucinda was thankful that Marcia Henley had seen her run naked to the staging area. Marcia had guessed that Lucinda would be in big trouble arriving naked, unless it could be made to look normal. She found Carmen and two more of the females that shared the same barracks as they hurried to the staging area and convinced them to help save Lucinda's hide by stripping off their clothes.

When Captain Conley surveyed the troops in front of him, he saw five females completely naked standing close to one another. He turned to an aid close by him, his hand over the microphone. "Why are they naked? Bit unusual isn't it?"

"I believe they're all from the same barracks, must be a female bonding thing."

"I suppose you're right."

Marcia waited for Conley to speak and then whispered at Lucinda, "Nice red cheeks you got there."

"I was hoping no one would notice."

"Fat chance of that. I assume it was Mutton Head."

"Yeah. Damn siren, never got laid."

"Poor girl..." She laughed. "Maybe I can help you out there tonight." She reached for her hand. "Let me rephrase that, I will have you tonight. I got these girls to strip to save you from Conley's wrath and I will claim you tonight."

Lucinda looked at her, wondering how serious she was.

"I mean it, Lucinda. I've slept naked with you enough to know you want me too. I've been patient with you, but now it's time, even if I have to tie you up first." She gave Lucinda's hand a squeeze.

Lucinda squeezed her hand back. "Well, it won't be the first time tonight I got put in restraints."

Marcia listened to Conley describe the state of emergency, how the Alliance worlds were prepared to invade Praxton. It was going to be an interesting night between the invasion of Praxton and her conquest of Lucinda.

Chapter Six

The dinner guests at the embassy were Praxton citizens; the male being an owner of a large factory of clothing goods he wanted to export to Alliance worlds. He brought three females with him, with everyone sitting at a round table. One blonde female, wearing a thin yellow collar, watched Diane carefully. Diane noticed she looked younger than the rest, and had a leash attached from her collar to the back of the chair. Her yellow wrist cuffs were joined together with a short length of chain.

"But while I have been allowed to export most of my products, there is a ridiculous tariff placed on them. Tell me, Diane, as a representative of the Charter of Conduct Office and also part of the Alliance worlds, do you believe that is reasonable?"

Robert had a mixture of black and grey hair. He had a square jaw with dark brown eyes. He wore a formal suit, a blue jacket over a darker blue shirt that was left unbuttoned to show off a hairless chest.

"I'm sure, Master Robert that I cannot speak for the whole government or all the Alliance people, but if Praxton refuses to join the Alliance worlds, do you expect it would receive the same consideration as if it were? Other worlds pay a price to be part of the Alliance and one of the benefits they receive in return is a low tax on traded goods. If you want the same low tax, I would suggest joining the Alliance worlds is an excellent option."

His frown turned into a smile slowly. "Well said. I see why the Charter of Conduct Office sent you here. You represent them well."

"Tell me, Diane, how do you find a wearing collar and cuffs while here on Praxton?" Janice, a petite blonde with shoulder length hair, directed a question to move the conversation away from politics. She wore a dress made of white lace that made it obvious she wore nothing underneath, save for a spiral of metal around each breast that left the nipple exposed and pinched forward. Her black, wide, imitation leather collar matched the four cuffs and the belt around her waist. From the belt, black twisted cords went to each of the cuffs.

Diane felt everyone staring at her as she spoke. "To be honest, there isn't a simple answer for that. As fashion jewellery, I can get used to it. In some cultures on Alliance worlds, people pierce their bodies with jewellery. After a period of time, most will tell you they don't even notice it's there, or wouldn't be seen without it."

"What about the collar representing that a female belongs to a guardian?"

"I have a bit more trouble with that. All people should have the same rights. I don't feel comfortable being compelled to obey someone else's wishes."

"So you don't report to someone at the Charter of Conduct Office? You can do as you please?"

"That's different. To clarify, male and females should be treated the same."

"Do male and females use different public washrooms on Alliance worlds? Dress differently?"

"Well of course. But the washrooms are divided because men and women use the facilities differently. They dress differently because of choice. None are forced to be subservient." Diane wasn't going into a long explanation why washroom facilities were separated for men and women. On some Alliance worlds and on parts of Earth, the public washrooms were unisex at one time and on others, the washrooms were separated between the sexes with laws forbidding one gender from using the washroom of the other. The Charter of Conduct solution was a compromise. Male and females had separate toilet facilities, but shared the same sinks and washing area. The Charter of Conduct also recognized the difference in how men and women used the washroom and required that there be six toilets available to women for every five toilets or urinals available for men.

Praxton had established separate facilities for males and females. Praxton females were expected to devote a good part of their day to looking their best and their washrooms usually included chairs and viewscreens so they could spend the time to apply their make-up. Men generally had separate facilities that were a great deal simpler.

Lesley, a tall, slim brunette, spoke up. Her red satin dress consisted of two one-foot wide strips of cloth; one on the front with the other on the back, leaving her sides exposed and bare. The fabric pieces were joined together only at the shoulder and at the bottom at her thighs. Her collar and cuffs were also red with a red chain between her wrist cuffs and also between her ankle cuffs. "But that doesn't show you males and females are different? If a female on Earth allows a male to buy her dinner, lead her on the dance floor and then wear his ring, is that something that should be prevented by law? I wear Master Robert's collar because I want to. I can leave him at any time, if I follow the proper procedure." She turned to him and softly smiled, "I never will, you know."

"Okay, point taken. What I refer to is that females here don't have the same legal rights as males."

"True. But females, unlike males, aren't required to have a job. If a female commits a crime, her guardian is also responsible for her actions. So, I guess you could say we have different legal rights."

"That is what I was trying to point out. I understand what you are saying. Male and females are different and so are treated differently. But the Charter of Conduct Office believes everyone should have the same laws to work under."

Diane was glad that dessert was brought in, ending the discussion. She felt a bit pressured by the argument put forward by the women. It was obvious they liked Praxton the way it was and enjoyed the revealing fashions with restraints that went with it.

Ambassador LeBlanc proposed a toast of friendship and asked if they would like to go downstairs and sit in the courtyard.

"That sounds wonderful," Robert replied. He turned to Janice. "Please escort Irene and Lesley downstairs."

Diane watched as Janice took a leash, attached it to Lesley's collar and then gathered up the quiet Irene's leash. Diane noticed Robert's dark blue pants were loose fitting and with the fly a light mesh. She tried to see if he was wearing underwear, but his side was turned towards her.

Robert held up another leash. "Would you mind Mr. Ambassador?"

Diane watched Leblanc's eyes move from Robert's, to the leash and then to her. She suddenly understood. Robert wanted to escort her downstairs with the leash, and was asking permission from her supposed guardian. It was a situation she wasn't prepared for. If she refused, it could upset the relationship between Praxton and the Alliance worlds LeBlanc was trying so hard to achieve. If she accepted, it might look like she accepted the Praxton's way of life. She decided the relationship between worlds was more important than her comfort. She gave a small nod to LeBlanc.

"Of course Robert, by all means..." LeBlanc gave him a warm smile.

Diane stood as he first clipped the metal leash on her collar and joined her wrist cuffs together at her front. She looked down at her hands, surprised at his actions. She also had the opportunity to see his cock was exposed through the blue mesh.

Diane followed Robert out of the dining room to an elevator. The women all were staring at Diane, watching how she handled being on a leash. She tried to act as if it was a normal thing for her to do. Privately, she tried to keep her breathing even, but could feel her nipples press against the jewellery as they became engorged. She hoped the dress and the jewellery hid any sign of arousal.

Diane followed Robert outside on the patio where he hooked the end of the leash on a hook on one of the two large posts set in the ground. She recalled the posts were used on Reconciliation Day to display females as a welcome to guests. The other females were also hooked to the same post, save for Janice who appeared to be a senior female and therefore had greater privileges. Janice stayed with them however, when the two men took a stroll around the courtyard to talk after refreshments were served.

Diane used both her hands to take a drink as she stood with the other women, feeling a bit odd standing with the end of the leash loosely hooked on the post. She knew she didn't dare unhook it and walk around, deciding she might as well join in the conversation with the other women.

Janice soon asked her about Alliance world fashions and if the rumours of Praxton having an influence was true.

"Fashions, well I'm not always the best source of that. But uneven clothes are the latest trend, such as skirts with an uneven hemline. Tops would have an uneven bottom or at the collar. Also pants. The pants are already low cut, but some women take it to an extreme with an uneven waist that exposes even more. What some women do is wear a shirt and pants both with an uneven cut to show off one side."

"That sounds interesting. Maybe Robert can borrow that idea for his designs."

"There are also the skins for younger women. It's a strange, waxy like material that literally slides on. It looks like the pants are sprayed on and is so revealing that they sell modesty belts as an accessory. The belt has a centre piece that goes down to provide coverage between the legs."

"What about the Praxton fashions on Alliance worlds?"

"There are women who wear what looks like a collar, but without the lock and usually without the metal ring in the centre. Some also wear wrist cuffs, again without the locks. I guess some think of them as fashion accessories and may not even be aware of what they represent. I noticed some of the younger men have taken to wearing trousers with the decorated fly, but not with the see through mesh seen here."

Lesley giggled and said, "Too bad. Women have to expose their bodies for the sake of fashion, but the men continue to hide themselves. They wear big, flat shoes while we balance on these heels or go barefoot."

"Actually, one of the fashions I like here is the shoes. The shoes on Alliance worlds have a lower heel and are designed for quick on and off. These shoes make me taller and have more elaborate straps. It's more of a bother to put them on, but they look good."

"How about the collar and cuffs with the chains attached to them?" Janice asked.

"I guess I'm getting used to them. I'm also getting used to going without a bra, something I never thought would happen. Now, I'm not sure how I'll feel when I have to put one on again." She gave a bit of a shrug. "The collar and cuffs do add something to an outfit, but I could do without this leash." She touched the metal chain with her hand.

"You're not alone there. But you have to take the good with the bad. As soon as the men finish their great conversation and come back, I want to sit down."

Diane grinned. "Men do like to think themselves as being important, don't they?" She was beginning to have a feeling of belonging with the women.

Janice laughed, "Just minor ego problems."

Diane turned towards Irene. "How come she's so quiet?"

"Oh she's new with us and still a bit shy." Janice walked over to Irene, put her arm around her waist and first gave a hug and then a kiss on her cheek. "She'll be fine later." She then lifted up Irene's short dress and gave her a few quick smacks on her ass.

Diane had heard that a light smack on a female's bottom was considered a sign of affection. Still, it surprised her to see Irene quietly accept her dress being lifted and a pat on her cheeks. Diane also now knew she was the only one wearing panties and hoped the waist straps weren't too visible under her dress.

Irene saw Diane watching and gave her hesitant smile.

Diane moved closer to her.

"You're very pretty. I like your nipple jewellery."

Diane blushed slightly. "Thank you. Are you originally from Praxton?"

"Yes. I never have been off world. It sounds so different on Alliance worlds."

"Perhaps, but people are people no matter where you go."

"Do you have a guardian or a boyfriend?"

"No, I don't."

"A girlfriend...?"

"No, I just like men. I have girlfriends, but just as friends."

Irene lowered her voice. "I would like to kiss you."

Diane felt Irene's fingers walk along her arm. She was surprised by the proposition and didn't know what to do or say. Irene took Diane's silence to mean she wasn't refusing and suddenly leaned forward, kissing her on the lips, pushing forward as she separated her lips. Diane wasn't sure how to respond, but gave a kiss in return before stepping away. The other females didn't act as if what just transpired was abnormal, continuing their talk. To Diane's relief the men returned.

Janice led Irene and Lesley to a table while Robert led Diane behind them.

"If you don't have a commitment to another person, I would like you to consider wearing my collar." Robert indicated LaBlanc. "He has informed me he is only your acting guardian and are still free to choose a proper guardian."

"Your collar...?" Dianne was shocked by his directness.

"I want to be your guardian."

"Oh. Well, I will have to think about that."

Diane was almost speechless by his suggestion and was glad to be in the vicinity of the others as they sat down around the table. The server poured them a new round of drinks and set out a bowl of chips with various dips and cloth napkins. LeBlanc then dismissed her for the rest of the evening. The six of them continued to talk. Diane found the salty chips with the dip interesting, though it made her a bit thirsty for more of the alcoholic drink.

An hour later Robert indicated it was time to leave. He shook hands with LeBlanc and gave a Diane a kiss on her cheek. Each of his females gave her a hug as well as a kiss on the lips. Their guests left via the courtyard, disappearing through the gate at the back of the yard.

LeBlanc held out a chair for her to sit and took the end of her leash and attached it to the back of her chair. He whispered in her ear. "If I was your guardian, I would have given you a spanking right in front of the others."

Diane quickly turned her head and looked at him, her mouth open in surprise.

"Bare ass too for not showing proper respect to me."

He then sat down opposite of the small table, studying her reaction.

"Has your opinion changed towards Praxton?"

She was still a bit surprised by his suggestion of a spanking and blurted out the first thing that came to her mind. "Maybe a bit..." She took a drink using both her hands with the wrist cuffs still joined together. "Are you going to keep my wrists locked together?" Her eyes also went to the leash that went to the back of her chair, trying to keep the topic away from spanking.

"Perhaps a while longer." He took a sip of his brandy. "Have some more wine." He poured wine from the decanter into her glass.

She questioned him with her eyes and then took another swallow of the wine.

"You know, Diane, I've spent a long time in the political arena. There is a lot of posturing and bluffing. People don't always say exactly what they mean."

"I suppose that is true even outside of politics."

"Indeed. You stated your views of Praxton society quite strongly when you first arrived, views that no doubt reflected those of the Charter of Conduct Office. However, I was impressed on how well you supported my efforts to bridge relations with our Praxton guests by acting out the role of a Praxton female. It must have been quite an ordeal for you."

Diane wet her lips before speaking, trying to be careful with her words as the wine affected her thinking. "I did what I thought was best. I admit I was a bit uncomfortable at first. I suppose I did get use to the collar and the submissive demeanour expected of females here."

He picked up a cloth napkin, rolling between his hands. "May I indulge in a bit of fantasy and a bit of what if?"

"Go ahead." Diane felt her heart beat faster, wondering what he was up to.

"Let us suppose for the moment that you were a true Praxton female."

"Alright."

"Now, because you are wearing my collar, I have certain rights." He paused to let her reflect on what he said. "I was thinking that this napkin would make a fine gag. It is soft enough not to hurt your mouth, but thick enough to stifle sounds."

She studied the napkin, trying to decide if he was seriously considering gagging her or not. "I suppose it would make a good gag. I guess that leads to the question why you would want to."

"Because after tying the gag I would undo your dress. If I'm not mistaken, one zipper at the back and the dress would simply fall to the floor. Of course, I would also remove any panties you might be wearing as well."

Diane looked at her cuffed wrists, realizing if he decided to do as he proposed, she wouldn't be able to stop him. "I see. Then where does flight of fantasy take you?"

"You'd be naked, gagged and cuffed, in other words helpless and vulnerable to my wants. Perhaps I would take you to the discipline room. I could put you in one of the cages and keep you there for later use." He watched her eyes carefully as he spoke.

Diane felt her pulse quicken as he spoke. She swallowed hard as she took another drink of her wine. She knew she was getting more aroused as LeBlanc spoke of what he wanted to do to her and felt he could see that in her face. "Well that's an interesting fantasy, but I think it's getting late."

"Of course. You must be getting tired. But I was curious to your reaction to my scenario. It does assume you are a Praxton female, and I am your guardian." He stood and then moved to her chair and picked up the end of the leash.

Diane stood and followed him inside the building. Her eyes looked down the hall where the discipline room was located as he lead her to the elevator.

He looked where she was staring. "The discipline room isn't far from here."

She quickly averted her eyes to where the elevator waited. "Not tonight." She squeezed her eyes closed at her mistake, knowing her answer implied another time.

They rode up in silence and he escorted her to her suite where he undid her wrist cuffs from each other.

"You didn't give me an answer of what you thought about my scenario."

She studied him a few seconds. "If I was a Praxton female, then I would say I would find your scenario acceptable, but as we know I'm not a Praxton female."

He nodded and slowly leaned forward and gave her a gentle kiss on her lips. "Have a good sleep, Diane." He placed the napkin in her hand. "A memento of tonight..." He turned to leave.

She clutched the napkin. "What about the locks on the collar and cuffs? You have the keys."

LeBlanc spoke. "Come and see me in the morning."

She stared back at him. "So that's how it is. What about the leash? Do you want it back later as well?"

"Ah, the leash. Why don't you leave it attached tonight and hook it on the end of your bed. It will give you the experience on how many Praxton females sleep."

She watched him walk down the hall and then turned and entered her room, feeling as if her world had been turned upside down. She unzipped her dress, watched it slide to the floor and imagined it was LeBlanc who had done it. Diane pulled her panties and nipple jewellery off as she stood in front of the viewscreen, watching herself. She slowly stretched the napkin and held it between her teeth, studying the image of a helpless female in front of her.

She sighed, placing the napkin on the bedside table and removed her shoes, thinking about the small kiss and his suggestions. She shut the lights off and hooked the end of the leash on a convenient hook at the corner of the bed before lying on her back. She rested her hands on her chest, the small chains from her collar to her cuffs restricting where she could place them.

Damn it Troy, this just isn't fair.

* * * *

As Diane dressed, she pondered what to wear. After an internal debate, she went with a white transparent blouse with a set of nipple jewellery that was joined by a chain. The jewellery was hollow in the centre and accented her nipples rather than covered them. She then put on one of her new Praxton skirts. She left the short chains from her collar to her wrist cuffs on, as well as the leash to her collar. The other end of the leash she held in her hand.

Diane knocked on the door of the ambassador's office, entering on his acknowledgment.

"Good morning, Diane. Did you sleep well?"

"Once I fell asleep I did." She sat down on the chair in front of his desk. She did what she saw other Praxton females do when wearing a short flared skirt and let the back of the black skirt drape behind her.

"Have you come to have the locks undone?" He held up a key.

She ignored his question. "You had me confused last night, Troy."

"How so...?"

"You described what you would do if I was a Praxton female. After that you took me back to my suite."

He nodded.

"Then you refused to unlock my collar and cuffs and told me to hook the leash on the end of the bed. You treated me like I was a Praxton female at that point."

"So you kept the leash attached to the collar and hooked it to the bed?"

"I assumed it was an order, not a request. So I obeyed it." She tried to look defiant at him. "So now I'm wondering, are you trying to make me a Praxton female? Are you trying to be my guardian? Because I'm not ready for that. I am still a Charter of Conduct Office representative. I was being polite last night, so don't think I'm giving in to Praxton philosophy." Diane raced out the words in her last statement, her composure shaken.

"I understand what you are saying." He twisted the key in his fingers. "Allow me to undo your locks. However, in two days' time I'm scheduled to be hosting another of Praxton's social elite. Of course, the ultimatum will have passed by then, but the Alliance military may not have launched an attack yet. Even if they do, they will not strike at cities unless an attack comes from one. In any case, the Praxton population wants to carry on as normally as possible. They are a determined people, and probably will want the dinner to take place. I was hoping you would attend as well. You represented the Charter of Conduct Office position quite well."

"Thank you." Diane was surprised by his compliment. "Yes, I suppose I could attend."

"Excellent." He walked around his desk and used the key to unlock the collar and cuffs. "Of course, I will ask Carol Miller to find you appropriate attire for the occasion."

"Will that include locked collar and cuffs with you keeping both keys again?"

"The customs on Praxton are long standing. Do you mind if I hold the keys?"

"No, if it makes you feel better. Just make sure the collar and cuffs are unlocked at the end of the night this time."

He chuckled. "I promise you I will treat you with the utmost respect."

She left his office knowing he hadn't given her any assurance he would remove the locks at the end of the evening.

She found herself fantasizing LeBlanc kissing her in his office, pressing on her lips as she opened her mouth. He then turned her around so she faced forward against the wall, lifting her skirt and spanking her.

"Diane!"

Diane turned in the hallway and saw Carol Miller approaching her from behind.

"Hey, I called you three times. Mind somewhere else?"

"Umm, yes, a report I have to do."

"Oh, I just wanted to know if you have time for a drink in the lounge."

"Sure, I'll make the time." She looked closely at Carol who was looking excited and ready to explode with news.

* * * *

Troy LeBlanc closed his office door and opened a cabinet door, removing a bottle of Praxton brandy to pour a drink. He immediately took a drink and then topped off the glass again. He pondered his dilemma, wondering how far he could go and if he had enough time to accomplish what he wanted. He had been the ambassador for four years and in that time he had received high praise from his superiors for his ability to mend fences after the disaster his predecessor had left behind. The former ambassador had infuriated the Praxton government and business leaders with his refusal to accept any of the social customs and culture of Praxton. The Alliance government wanted to avoid war and had hoped the Charter of Conduct could be introduced and finally accepted by the Praxton government. However, the former ambassador had alienated all of his planetary contacts.

LeBlanc was told to try a different approach and when he was first was able to hold meetings and receptions, his Alliance superiors were elated that progress was being made. But LeBlanc was a troubled man in his new role. His companion of three years had refused to go with him to Praxton, citing concerns about her own career and that she *"refused to be kept like a pet"*. At first, he didn't mind the break up, thinking they weren't really suited for each other in the long run with both wanting to pursue careers. But when he arrived on Praxton, he found himself to be excluded from most females. Freelancers were available, but it didn't look good for the ambassador to be seen with them. The embassy staff was also difficult, since he was a superior to them all and it might be perceived he was taking advantage of them. Praxton women were numerous and usually very good looking, however all the females he met wore a collar. That meant they were already under the care of a guardian, and he was reluctant to try to take a female from one of the leaders of Praxton. Troy LeBlanc became very lonely. Worse still, he found the collars and cuffs on the women enticing. He craved to have a female wearing his collar and wondered what it would be like to discipline a female.

Until recently, it was all a fantasy. True he had changed the downstairs to something more likely found on Praxton, but he managed to explain that to his superiors as a place where Praxton visitors felt at home. He firmly stated they were for show only.

Then Diane showed up and his world changed. At his insistence, she reluctantly agreed to wear a collar to travel outside the embassy to visit Teri Baxter. He lied to her that she was unable to leave a short time later due to the emergency and slowly tried to introduce her to collars and bondage. To his astonishment, she began to accept the role of a Praxton female. It was more than he had dared to hope for. He carefully laid plans that would push her a bit more each time to what he desired, while at the same time he desperately tried to find a way Praxton society could exist under the Charter of Conduct.

He knew home office was now apprehensive of him and had politely inquired on how he was coping. Despite their suspicions, they also had indicated they were pleased he was still able to have the Praxton officials negotiate for implementing the Charter of Conduct. If the negotiations failed, he had no doubt he would be sent home in disgrace for accepting the Praxton position. But if the negotiations were successful, they would give him the benefit of the doubt, applauding his unusual methods.

He still wondered if his ultimate goal of her complete surrender to him was attainable. He had laid the groundwork, now he had to wait and see.

* * * *

In the lounge, Carol started talking to Diane before their drinks even arrived.

"I was thinking about what you said earlier, about following your heart. I figured you were right. Falling in love isn't predictable when and where it happens. I love Gordon and I don't know when, if ever, I'll meet another man like him. So, I called him late last night and we talked about this and that. Then he said, 'You know my offer of being your guardian is still open.' I froze there for a moment and asked if he really meant that. He said, 'Of course.' I couldn't help myself. I started to cry and then said yes!" Carol looked at Diane with her eyes wet with emotion.

Diane gave her a grin. "Congratulations Carol. When is the big day that it becomes official?"

"That may be a while yet with Alliance ultimatum. I'm still an Alliance citizen and have to apply to immigrate to Praxton before we can sign a guardian contract. But I have even more news."

"What is that?"

"Well, I went to see Ambassador LeBlanc to tell him about my decision about immigrating to Praxton and accepting Gordon as my guardian. He didn't seem too surprised and wished me the best of luck. Then, well, next you know he's asked you to attend a dinner tomorrow night?"

"Yes, another important Praxton guest."

"Right, real important. This is the deputy minister of the Praxton armed forces. Ambassador LeBlanc is trying any diplomatic avenue he can find to avert war and so he is meeting a lot of people. He looks so stressed from the situation. Anyway, this Carl Stewart is well up there in the political arena so Ambassador LeBlanc needs to present the best image of the Alliance worlds he can. This Stewart guy has real strong views on the Praxton culture so Ambassador LeBlanc asked me if I would accept being a fille d'affichage."

"A what...? Fille d'affichage is French isn't it?"

"It is. It means something like female on display and it's used on special occasions. A female is put in restraints where guests are gathered and is left there during the evening."

"Isn't that a little hard on her? I'm guessing she's naked as well."

"Right. She's usually gagged as well. Because she can be in restraints for a long time, they often use cloth to hold her to be easier on her skin. I was surprised the Ambassador asked me. It's quite an honour."

"I guess all I can say is congratulations a second time."

"I just have to work out how I want to be positioned."

Diane was a bit surprised at how much Carol looked forward to being put naked into restraints in front of others. "I'm sure whatever position you pick you will look fine."

"Thank you. It's an honour for you to be included in this dinner you know. The Ambassador must have liked how you did at the last dinner."

"He didn't really say."

"Well he's asking you for one of the most important private dinners held here in a long time. By the way, he is hoping you will again respect Praxton customs regarding females for this event as well."

"I will do as he asks for the sake of Praxton and Alliance relations." Diane took a quick drink from her glass, thinking about the collar and leash she wore last time. "I assume he will be keeping the keys with him again and I have to wear a leash."

"Yes he did mention that."

"I better try and find something to wear then."

"Oh, the Ambassador said that apparently you admired a white dress that a female wore at the last dinner, so he asked Master Robert if he could send a copy of it for you to wear."

Diane recalled the white lace dress that Janice wore that didn't hide any of her body or the fact she wore nothing underneath. "That was quite a revealing dress."

"Don't be like that." Carol wagged her finger at her. "The deputy minister will note that you are wearing a Praxton dress and will be pleased about that."

"Alright then I'll wear it, but I'll feel as exposed as you will be."

Carol grinned. "But it will be fun. I think Ambassador LeBlanc really likes you. Being an Alliance citizen, he is in a difficult position if he wants to have Praxton female companions. You are a bit of a challenge for him, so I think he finds you interesting in a lot of ways."

Diane blushed. "I don't know about that."

"Don't be silly, of course he does. By the way, I'll stop at your suite tomorrow afternoon and help you get ready for the dinner. You're still new at the way Praxton females prepare."

Diane did as Carol suggested and took a warm bath and relaxed in the water with bubbles and skin oils in it. She put on the thin housecoat and read, occasionally glancing at the white lace dress lying on her bed that was more transparent than she remembered from before. Next to the dress, a package containing a collar and various restraints also occupied her interest. Carol knocked on her door, breaking into her thoughts.

Diane let her in, noticing she wasn't wearing much either in anticipation of being put in restraints later. Carol wore a simple white shirt with a large open back and a short skirt that barely covered the bottom of her cheeks while standing.

Diane sat naked as Carol explained the different types of makeup plus how and where to apply them. "Always use this last and lightly brush it on. It stops the makeup from coming off your skin and on to the clothing. It also adds a bit of sheen to the skin. Now for the jewellery. You won't want to wear much as this dress really is meant to show off your body, but I have this nice silver nipple set."

Diane looked at the two round pincher devices connected by a chain. "Those look like they might hurt."

"Just a bit, but you'll get use to them." Carol opened one set and placed it behind the nipple. "It pinches your nipple forward and helps make it stand out behind the dress."

Diane winced. "It better do a lot of good. That hurts."

"The pain will go in a minute." She attached the other set. "Some sets like these come with a locking mechanism, so the guardian can use the chain that runs between them to guide the female instead of a leash."

"I'd rather have a leash."

Diane pulled her dress on, finding it a bit tight. She did up a series of buttons along one side, leaving a few undone near the bottom to make walking easier. There were also buttons on her shoulder and she looked at them questioningly.

"The dress, like many on Praxton, is designed so they can be removed even if the female's hands are cuffed together," Carol replied.

"Some dresses can fall apart on a single pull of a string."

Diane nodded, putting on her collar and leash. Carol then secured the locks on her cuffs and collar.

"There, you're all set except for your shoes. Good luck on your dinner date." She grinned. "Oh, one other thing, this Deputy Minister is a bit of a disciplinarian, so try not to be shocked how he talks, like the use of spankings."

"He might spank his females in front of me?"

"Yeah, and he might expect the Ambassador to do the same to you."

"You're kidding, I hope."

"You can handle it. You're already dressed like a Praxton female. This is just one more step. The spankings aren't hard, and you may even enjoy it. I do when Gordon spanks me."

Diane closed her eyes. "The barbarians are at the doors."

Carol laughed. "I gotta go." She gave Diane a hug and a kiss. "Have fun." She then gave Diane several light smacks on her ass and turned to leave.

Diane was surprised at first before remembering Praxton females gave their friends a light spanking. "Thanks, and I hope you have fun too. See you later."

"Yeah, all of me."

Diane looked in the mirror after she finished dressing, noticing her nipples were very evident due to the jewellery pushing them forward.

* * * *

Troy LeBlanc escorted Diane to the private dining room, carrying the metal chain leash loosely in one hand. She noticed he kept glancing at her body that was quite visible under her dress.

"This Carl Stewart is a bit rough around the edges, pushes hard. I hope to persuade him to carry our argument to the Minister of Defence that accepting the Charter of Conduct need not be the end of Praxton culture. He may decide to see your reaction to some things done on Praxton."

"I will do what I can. I feel I have already done a lot in that regard by wearing this dress and collar, not to mention this leash. If that wasn't quite enough you kept the keys to the locks. I can't even take off this belt without your permission."

"It is the Praxton way."

"Carol warned me there may be spankings tonight."

"Yes, there could well be."

"Does that supposedly include me?"

"He may expect me to show that I'm in control as well."

"Then I suppose I will have to be prepared to be spanked by you." She looked at him. "It will be humiliating, but I'm willing to do this to help negotiations. Of course, with these restraints I'm wearing, I doubt you need my permission anyway. You certainly could do so any time you wanted."

"Thank you for your understanding in this matter."

"Ambassador, I'm simply trying my best to accommodate your wishes to help the Alliance cause."

He held open the door to the dining room. "Shall we go in and wait for   our   guests?"

Chapter Seven

The soldiers dispersed, talking about what the captain had announced. The Alliance forces had given notice they were extending the deadline for compliance with the Charter of Conduct by forty-eight hours. After that, an attack could commence at any time.

The Praxton soldiers were prepared to use their training in a real combat situation. Tomorrow morning they would line up and find out what their individual missions would be. Marcia patted Lucinda on her ass and then grabbed her hand as the assembly broke.

"Pretty exciting, Lucinda."

"Yeah, going to be tough to sleep tonight..."

"I bet you'll sleep real well after I'm through with you. You're not escaping from me tonight."

"How about a rain check instead?"

"How about I tie you up and have my way with you instead?"

"Marcia ..."

"One more word of protest and you'll get a spanking as well."

Lucinda looked at her friend and let out a sigh. "Okay, I guess I owe it to you for getting the rest of the females to strip to save my ass."

"That's not the reason I want to hear. I want you to want to have sex with me because you want to. We have been bunk beds for a long time, kissed each other, touched each other and now it's time for the next step."

"You're right. I'm just nervous about it, that's all. I want to, I do. I'm just scared a bit. I never did it with another female before."

Marcia put her arm around Lucinda's waist as they walked and gave her a hug. "Don't worry. I'll be careful with you."

Lucinda could hear that a lot of the other females were celebrating with each other. Some were talking and laughing. Others were taking advantage of possibly the last night they would spend together. Lucinda rested on her side as Marcia stroked her cheek and kissed her on her forehead. She followed with more kisses on her face and on her lips. Lucinda responded by kissing Marcia back and they held each other in each other's arms. Marcia dropped down, kissing her neck and her breasts. Lucinda moaned lightly.

"Relax, just relax." Marcia placed her mouth over each nipple, working with her tongue as she sucked on them. "Why don't you roll onto your back?"

Lucinda rolled on her back as Marcia continued to kiss her. Slowly, Marcia slid her hand downward and between Lucinda's legs. As she sucked on a nipple, she slowly massaged Lucinda's pussy with her fingertips.

"That feels so good Marcia."

"It's going to feel even better soon." Marcia lowered her head and went between Lucinda's legs. She licked at Lucinda's pussy, pushing her tongue between her lips.

Lucinda closed her eyes, the noise from the other females faded away. Marcia's kissing, licking and touching her was causing her to lose control. She dug her fingers into the bed sheets as she arched her back. A few seconds later, she let out a cry as she climaxed.

Lucinda became aware of the world around her and suddenly realized some of the other females were applauding with encouraging shouts. She wondered what the cheering was about and then realized the comments were directed at her.

"Oh no, Marcia. Did I make a lot of noise when, that is did I scream or something?"

Marcia laughed. "Well, you did let us all know you came."

"I'm so embarrassed."

"Don't be. I wanted you and the sound you made was very satisfying."

Marcia held Lucinda in her arms. "Now you need to get some rest for the big day tomorrow."

Lucinda kissed Marcia. "Thank you. I will sleep well tonight."

In the morning, they lined up for inspection and then were given their assignment sheets. Lucinda looked at names on her list and found that Eric Winston was in the same group.

"Marcia, look." She pointed at his name on the list.

"Oh that'll make you happy."

Lucinda just grinned.

They walked hand in hand to get breakfast when they heard a male voice call out Lucinda's name. They turned around to see Eric jogging up to them.

"Hey, I see we're on the same team." Lucinda gave him a grin.

"Yeah, I saw that too. Good thing, we have unfinished business."

"Is that so?"

Marcia spoke to both of them. "I'll save some seats for you two inside. Just don't get into fight."

Eric waited until Marcia was out of hearing range. "We didn't get to complete our task."

"No we didn't. Emergency sirens can spoil an evening."

He took her hand. "I've got to ask you something."

"What?"

"You asked me to put handcuffs on you. So I was wondering if what you were really saying is that you want me to take control of you?"

"And if I am?"

"Then I would like to collar you."

Lucinda looked to the ground and back up to him. "I would very much like to wear your collar."

"Then I shall claim you after this Alliance world conflict is over."

Lucinda looked around to see if anyone was watching them and gave Eric a quick kiss. "I hope the conflict doesn't take long then."

Marcia held two chairs for them at the table. She looked at Lucinda's grinning face and laughed. "Someone sure looks happy."

"Eric wants to collar me!"

Eric nodded. "As soon as the conflict is over."

"Well congratulations. So are you going to wear two collars or are you going to leave the service?"

Females in the military service wore the military collar during on duty time, but could switch to another collar during the other times.

"I don't know. We didn't get that far yet. Whatever Eric feels is best."

Eric smiled. "If after this conflict you want to remain in the service, then that's fine with me. Just don't get promoted above me."

Lucinda laughed. "Yes sir."

* * * *

Terri checked her messages, noticing each one was coming only from within Praxton. The Alliance military had stopped incoming and outgoing messages to the planet, making everyone on Praxton feel isolated. She was about to reply to one message when a new one popped in. Terri looked, surprised that it was from her friend Mila from somewhere on an Alliance world.

Terri! Roland has found a sneaky way to be able to send messages to you. I told you he works on space communications, a network relay engineer. Anyway, he can bypass the normal safeguards and get messages through what he calls the back door, something about using a test sequence code.

How have you been? Things are great here. Roland has gotten really dominant since we got back. Last week he held up my collar before I was about to leave for work and told me I had to wear it.

I put it on and then he locked it! It was an interesting conversation piece at work, but Praxton collars and stuff are the latest fashion accessories so I got away with it. But the collar was just the start of it. He gave me a good spanking that evening as well!

I have to ask you a favour. Roland and I were fooling around and he decided he wanted to capture me. He tied my hands behind my back and took out the old playpen we had and turned it upside down over me. It was interesting, very interesting, because he could reach into the playpen and I couldn't do anything. So, the favour I want to ask, if you can ship me one of those collapsible cages when this conflict is over. I'll pay you for it of course. It's just that it's hard to order Praxton goods from here at the best of times, let alone now. I know it's going to take a while, but I'm looking forward to being in a proper cage and not one with cartoon figures on the inside!

There is a trick to sending me a message back. I have attached

Roland's multiplex compression encryption software. So after making up a message, you have to compress it using his software and then send it. The software automatically reroutes it as a test message and then it goes to me.

Love Mila

Terri was thankful that at least planet wide communication was still available, but how long that would last was anyone's guess. She sent a message to Karen DuPont, a friend who ran a tourist zone historical information theatre, outlining what she wanted to do. She flagged the message as urgent and then she went downstairs from her room to where Romie was watching the latest news. She walked slowly, the chain that ran between her ankle cuffs made her conscious of each step she took.

After Romie allowed her to remain in the household after her trial, she decided to wear what he liked, which was both cuffs and chains. She didn't mind wearing cuffs on her wrists and ankles, but the added chains hampered some of her movement. Terri knew she had disappointed him and it was only because of the intervention on her behalf by Tam and Anne that he decided she could stay in his house. Romie had gradually removed her restrictions, and soon she was allowed to carry on much as before in her travels outside the home. But she was very careful around him, showing that she was properly submissive in her movements, posture and wearing chains.

She entered the room and sat on her knees by his side on the floor, spread her legs slightly and then rested her hands on her lap. She waited for him to turn towards her. Before she presented herself to him she also made sure she dressed exactly as he liked, wearing a white sheer top with the new skirt style that had an open weave along one side. The design of skirt meant she had to go without panties so the side of the skirt showed only skin.

He finally acknowledged her. "Yes Terri?"

"Master Romie, I have a plan to help Praxton against the Alliance worlds."

He studied her for a few seconds, then asked, "How so?"

"I was thinking that we can create a video explaining Praxton society and send it out to the Alliance worlds. The video would promote

Praxton way of life including females happily submitting to their guardians. We can do the video where Karen works. She has agreed we can use her facilities."

"That is fine to do a video, but the Alliance government has stopped all off world communication and has resisted my efforts to send out pro-Praxton videos in the past. So I don't see how doing a video will help us."

"My friend Mila's partner, Roland, works as a Global Communication engineer. After they shut down outside communication, she was able to send me a message asking me if I was alright. Roland knows of a diagnostic code that allows him to bypass the block. I sent her a message back and asked if she could help us send out a video. We can flood the Alliance worlds with a video and that might stop their attack if the propaganda that we are slaves is refuted."

"You're sure you can get a video out?"

Terri nodded. "Mila said she could and she has a lot of Alliance world contacts. It would spread pretty fast."

"I suppose it would be worth a try."

"We can use Karen's facilities to make the video and I was wondering if you would produce it?"

"That is a definite possibility. It will at least give us something to do while we're waiting."

* * * *

Karen DuPont stood facing over two dozen females and the six men. She began to speak. "Thank you all for coming and agreeing to help out making our video. Some of you may be nervous. That's okay. We want to show a natural look and if some of you are excited or nervous or even bored, that fits in what we want to show too."

She gestured behind her. "This is the stage area where we will do everything. The stage can generate a lot of special effects, including holograms that can be very realistic. Remember these are holograms. You cannot be hurt if you fall off the edge of a building or whatever hologram image is being generated."

She turned towards a tall dark skinned man, holding a riding crop in his hand. "Master Gary is the director of the show and will now speak to you of what is required."

He stood for several seconds before speaking, looking at the group in front of him. "We have some restrictions on what we can do. The video has to be done quickly and without any large funds to support it. I need all of you ladies to follow my instructions during the production. Those who don't will feel the sting of my whip here. To make this production work, I'm quite prepared to be harsh."

He walked up to the closest female and hooked a finger through the ring in her blue metal collar. The brunette peered at him and walked without resistance as he pulled her to the front of the stage.

"What is your name?"

"Corrine, Master Gary."

"Are you willing to do your part in this video to help Praxton?"

"Yes, Master Gary?"

"Even personal discomfort.?"

"Yes, Master Gary."

"Good, I see we have reached an understanding. Corrine, thank you. You may join the others."

Corrine hurried back to join the others.

Gary paced a few steps back and forth and then spoke. "I'm taking this video very seriously. I expect you to do so as well. Karen will now give you some more directions. We will be starting in exactly one hour."

He walked off the stage briskly, and Karen waited until he left to speak.

"Okay, please listen up. We will meet here in thirty minutes. Everyone, including the men, will be given different clothes to wear. We are going to show some of our shopping centres and daytime activity. Then we are going to do a Praxton fashion show and a feature on some of the fashion accessories. We want the show to be exciting and a Praxton fashion show will certainly do that. Okay, we don't have much time. Thirty minutes."

She walked back stage to where Gary was sitting, looking at material on his notebook. He looked up.

Well, do you think I inspired them enough to take this seriously?"

"Definitely."

He chuckled. "Well, at least that part of the plan worked. I was worried they would think this too much of a fun thing. Most of those females were supposed to be used to cameras too. Let's hope the video works as well."

"Everything should be fine. By the way the producer Romie Crocetti got Black Steel to agree to redo his video of *Strike Her!*, using Terri Baxter. We'll put that in the video package as well."

"That's a good plan. The video is very popular here and I've heard that there is a lot interest in the video from Alliance world tourists."

Thirty minutes later, they began the video using a holographic simulation of a shopping mall. The camera focused on the happy females shopping, stopping at a coffee shop and then at a lounge. Some of the females were with male guardians and two of them had leashes attached to their collars. Close-ups of different collars and cuffs worn were videoed as well as display cases that showed the collars as jewellery.

The simulated mall also featured a fashion show. The latest in Praxton fashions that emphasised the unique clothing women wore was videoed. Cuffs and matching collars complementing the dresses, skirts and tops were highlighted, along with the high-heeled footwear. Male fashions with the partially open weave fly were also shown, along with the male heavy boots and open front shirts.

Romie came by to talk to Gary and Karen, asking how the video was proceeding.

"Very well. Karen has recruited some excellent people for this video."

"Good. When you're done with the mall sequence, I want you to do a video at a nightclub. Show some drinking, dancing and perhaps a bit of female nudity. We want people to seek out this video and they will when they hear that it has nudity. From the nightclub scene, we will introduce Black Steel's music video. Terri is meeting with him now to work out the details and they will arrive here this afternoon. I know this is making you squeeze in a lot of shooting in a short time, but we don't have the luxury of doing this letter perfect."

"No worries. We'll get it done. I have a good software engineer that will help fix up some minor glitches as well. I'm looking forward to watching Black Steel perform, especially with Terri as one of the bad females."

Romie chuckled. "She does manage to project that doesn't she?"

Chapter Eight

Diane entered the large rectangular dining room. The table with the dozen chairs around sat at the front, near the door. Behind the table, a large metal C shaped device stood with a large circular base. The top rose eight feet above the floor and held a metal box where strips of cloth hung from a group of hooks.

The cloth strips were made of a white, semi-transparent material attached to a naked Carol. Different pieces of cloth were wrapped around her body with separate cloths for each limb as well a length of cloth around her torso. In addition, she was blindfolded as she lay suspended horizontally with her arms tied above her head.

LeBlanc led Diane past the table and to where Carol slowly swayed under the strips of cloth.

"Our guests won't be here for a few minutes yet so why don't you converse with Carol? Let her know she looks good as this is her first time at being on display."

Diane nodded as she gazed at Carol. She looked aroused with full nipples as she twisted against her restraints, looking sensual as she stretched out her body in front of her. She took a few final steps and stopped next to Carol.

"Hi Carol, you look wonderful."

"Diane? Thanks, I don't know how I look."

"You look very sexy."

LeBlanc leaned towards Diane and whispered in her ear. "On Praxton it is customary for females that are friends of the fille d'affichage to touch and kiss her. It is an acknowledgment that she looks beautiful. Since a fille d'affichage is often blindfolded and feels isolated from those in the room, she will enjoy being touched." He traced a finger from Carol's chin down to her breast. "I will return in a few minutes. I have to make sure everything is in order."

Diane watched him and then turned her attention back to Carol. She assumed she wasn't allowed to leave Carol's side; LeBlanc had left her there after leading her there by the leash. He had already alluded to a possible spanking, and she didn't want to give him an easy excuse to give her one.

"So are you comfortable this way?"

"So far. These cloths don't pull on my skin like a rope would and I can move my limbs as well." She drew up her legs at her knees. "I guess this isn't what I thought how I was going to be displayed, but I still feel I look erotic."

"You do." Diane remembered LeBlanc telling her a fille d'affichage liked to be touched and placed a hand on her rib cage. "How did you think they were going to display you?"

Carol licked her lips. "I thought they were going to suspend me by my wrists, maybe separate my legs as well." Carol gave a small gasp as she felt Diane's hand slide up to the bottom of her breast. "I also heard that sometimes they tie a rope around your waist and then tie loose end between your legs. Sometimes they will put a knot or a vibrating device on the crotch rope." She moaned as Diane covered her breast with her hand and began to work the erect nipple.

Diane watched her hand massage Carol's breast. She felt like she was in complete control over Carol, could do anything she wanted to her. It was a feeling of power over another individual and she suddenly understood the attraction of Praxton females to men. Why Praxton females enjoyed the dominance of their guardian. "So you wanted to have a crotch rope on?" she demanded.

"I, I heard…it gives pleasure and makes the female feel… oh God that feels good," Carol gulped air as Diane placed her mouth over her nipple and teased it with her tongue. "Makes the female feel she's under control… that her guardian will decide when she comes. I was… curious how… it felt."

Diane lifted her head and looked at the obviously aroused Carol who was gasping for breath. The feeling of controlling Carol was arousing for her as well and she bent down to kiss Carol deeply. Diane broke off the kiss and looked at Carol as she struggled in her restraints, her arms twisting above her head and with the leg closest to her drawn up. Diane took her open palm and smacked Carol on her ass as she thought, *I own you completely. I can do what I want to you.*

"Oh!"

"You like that, don't you?" Diane suddenly on impulse reached between Carol's legs, finding her wet.

"I do, I do."

Diane heard LeBlanc come into the room and quickly moved her hands away from Carol. "I will see you later, and maybe I'll finish what I started."

"Have you kept Carol company while I was gone?"

"Yes Ambassador LeBlanc."

"Good." He took the end of Diane's leash and led her to the table. "I will sit you here. You may not get up without permission, understood?"

Diane nodded. "Yes Ambassador." Diane sat down, thinking it was odd how submissive she felt to LeBlanc after her power trip over Carol.

LeBlanc hooked her leash behind her chair and sat next to her. "Our guests will be here momentarily. You will be the subject of some interest by the Deputy Minister as he is understandably suspicious of anyone from Alliance worlds."

"I will try not to disappoint you, Ambassador, or Charter of Conduct Office."

A minute later LeBlanc greeted the deputy minister and five females. One female was in charge of the others, leading the others as they entered the room.

The group accepted wine from LeBlanc and then walked around the room, admiring Carol as she slowly moved her limbs against the restraints. LeBlanc took Diane's leash and led her around.

Carl Stewart approached Diane and commented on Carol. "Isn't she a lovely sight? Like a living piece of art."

Diane looked at how Carl carried himself. His light blue suit making his broad shoulders look even bigger. His pants had an over-sized fly made of a white mesh that showed that he had a design of red and blue tattooed on his cock.

"She is beautiful." She tried not to gaze too long at his member and averted her eyes to LeBlanc who stood close by nervously listening to the conversation. "I guess art is still in the eye of the beholder."

"You don't find her in bonds attractive?"

"I didn't say that, merely whether this can be considered an art form."

"But by omission, you seem to be saying she looks beautiful in restraints."

Diane spoke carefully. "She looks beautiful in restraints, but that doesn't mean it is art or that it is right to do so."

"Do you deny she enjoys being naked and in restraints in view of us? We can ask her if you want."

"I don't refute that."

"Then if you enjoy looking at her as we do, then is there a problem with that?"

"I don't honestly know. Just because we all enjoy something, doesn't make it right. History is full of examples of groups of people of agreeing to a cause that is wrong. Cyper Seven, a few years ago, was of the opinion that harvesting the glour trees for their fruit was a good export item. Unfortunately, such harvesting would have disrupted the mating cycle of the cretal moth, perhaps to the point of making the blue tailed cretal moth extinct."

Stewart sighed. "We are not endangering any species this way are we?"

"No, only humanity. This is pleasure for us to be sure, but what of the long term consequences?"

Stewart walked away with a smirk on his lips. "At least you admit you find this pleasurable."

Diane opened her mouth for a retort, but then closed it, knowing she had been manoeuvred into agreeing she did find Carol in restraints pleasurable.

They sat down at the table and Diane looked at the dresses of the females. The senior female, Trina, sat next to Carl Stewart with the other females sitting in row next to her. Trina was blonde with a full figure and wore a navy blue top over a white skirt. Her wrists cuffs and collar were also white with a silver chain running between the collar and the cuffs. Next to her, a brunette was dressed in a black lace dress. The slim female wore a wide black collar that was matched with wrist and ankle cuffs. In addition, she wore black restraints just above her elbows that were joined together at her back by a black coloured chain. She had barely enough reach to drink from her glass of wine.

The next two blonde females looked to be twins. Both were dressed the same in a light red flared skirt. From the skirt, two thin strips of cloth criss-crossed from the back to the front and barely covered their nipples. To complete their outfit, they wore red collars and the matching ankle and wrist cuffs were linked by chains to their belt. Diane looked at their C cup size breasts and was intrigued on how long before one of them popped out from under the cloth strips, either by accident or on purpose.

The last female, also a blonde, was the youngest looking and looked apprehensive in her sheer yellow top. The top was short, as well, and only held together by one clasp at the bottom. Her short brown skirt was tight fitting with a string on each side of the skirt holding it together in a zigzag pattern. Her wrists were cuffed together with a chain running from them to her metal collar.

Diane took a drink of her wine as she surveyed the others around the table, her eyes peering above the rim of her glass. They had been reviewing her as well and Diane felt self-conscious as the other females appraised her. She was pleased she wearing the white lace dress that was as revealing as that of the other females, not wanting to look out of place with the rest. While the other females all had nice bodies, Diane felt she had kept up her own looks. That came with the help of expensive cosmetic drugs, and being an officer of the Charter of Conduct Office, allowed her to purchase the heavily taxed drugs at a subsidy. She was aware that nipple clamps had made her nipples protrude and stand out under the lace material, drawing attention as she shifted in her chair that made her breasts move underneath.

"So Diane, are you enjoying your stay here on Praxton?"

"Yes I am Deputy Minister Stewart."

"I noticed that you are wearing the clothing and fashions of Praxton females. Don't you find this degrading to yourself and Alliance women?"

Diane smiled. "When in Rome? Whether such fashions as you call them are degrading is not for me to decide. That is for society to judge.

What the Charter of Conduct Office is concerned about, and by extension myself as one of their representatives, is if rights are ignored and people are forced to act against their wishes."

"So what rights do you see are being trampled here on Praxton?"

"Obviously women being held in restraints."

"I would say to you none of these women are forced to wear these restraints, that they wear them because they want to."

"If you are saying, that if we took a survey of the females on Praxton, and asked if they want to continue to wear restraints, I would agree that the vast majority would say yes. But I ask you, Deputy Minister Stewart, is it possible that the females on Praxton have been indoctrinated? I hesitate to use the term brain washed into believing restraints are a normal part of life. I ask this because if we ask the same question to females on Alliance worlds, the answer will be quite different."

Stewart chuckled. "Then one could argue the Alliance world females may be indoctrinated. You see, our population is growing on Praxton, in large part on the immigration from the Alliance worlds. Females apply to live here knowing full well of our lifestyle here. These women have been indoctrinated on Alliance customs, yet choose Praxton. They come here knowing they will be wearing collars, that they will be caged, spanked, whipped and forced to their knees. Very few choose to leave afterwards."

Diane took another drink of her wine, not sure how to respond. He was baiting her with reference to being caged, spanked, and whipped. She also knew what he meant by being forced to their knees, a not so subtle hint that females are expected to give males oral sex. She thought how Stewart had worn pants that allowed a view of his cock, like many males did on Praxton, letting the females around him know what was important. "People often want things that are not healthy for them. For example, there are drugs that are banned on all worlds, including Praxton. Just because some women crave to wear a collar and submit to men doesn't make it right."

"So we should force females to take roles they aren't comfortable with?"

"I didn't say or mean that."

"You're wearing a collar, cuffs and chains. If we assume you're intelligent and capable of resisting what you don't like, should we assume you enjoy wearing them?"

Diane took a deep breath in. She felt like she was being painted into a corner and was glad when the servers brought in the meal. She quickly began to eat her salad.

A few minutes later Stewart looked at her. "You didn't answer my question. Do you enjoy wearing the collar and cuffs?"

Diane knew it would look like a lie to say she didn't enjoy wearing them; she looked too comfortable with them on and it would be tough to explain why she was wearing them if she didn't want to. "I wear them to be part of Praxton society, but I also consider them as being worn as jewellery."

"Come now. They represent more than jewellery, damn it. They symbolize your submission to Ambassador LeBlanc. Your collar and cuffs are locked, and I would guess he holds the key. Do you deny his control over you?"

Diane pushed her empty salad bowl away. "Right now he is my superior as regulations stipulate for Charter of Conduct Office and Alliance Worlds."

"Bah! Regardless of the regulations is he in control of you?"

Diane refused to look at Stewart, averting her eyes to her plate. She began to eat off the main course set in front of her.

"Let me put it this way. If he ordered you to receive a spanking would you comply?"

Diane dropped her knife and fork and stared at him. "If it would make you happy and help Alliance and Praxton relations I would. If the only thing to make you make feel more comfortable with the Charter of Conduct Office purpose is for me to be spanked, then I'm willing to do so." She crossed her arms in defense.

"It will. After dessert will be fine."

Diane felt her stomach tighten. "Are you serious? You really want and need to see me spanked?"

"I do. I thought I made that clear. Are you willing to do it? Submit to Ambassador LeBlanc? If you do, I will request the Minister of Defence to meet with a representative of the Charter of Conduct Office."

"That is hardly fair. You won't put in the request if I refuse the spanking?"

"That's right. So what is your answer. Yes or no?"

"If that's what it takes, I will be glad to," Diane blurted out.

"Then it's settled. After dessert, which I understand is a fruit concoction, you will be spanked."

Diane opened her mouth and stared at him, and suddenly looked at LeBlanc, who was watching her with more than just curiosity in his eyes.

She felt trapped and wasn't sure how it happened. It occurred to her that perhaps that was what she really wanted to happen and allowed Stewart to manoeuvre her into that position. Diane felt she was smarter than the pompous Stewart yet lost a debate with him. It was as if she wanted the outcome for her to submit to Ambassador LeBlanc. She stared at the dessert placed in front of her, the swirled whipped topping holding her attention. She poked her fork into it and ate in silence, occasionally staring at the nude Carol twitching and looking erotic under her restraints.

I'm going to be spanked in front of these people, the thought kept repeating in her mind. She began to eat faster, her eyes trying to see everyone. Carol began to look more interesting to her, and she wondered if she was going to be stripped nude for her spanking. She wondered briefly if she could back out and refused to be spanked. *No, I have to go through with this. It will help the negotiations. I wish I knew why I feel excited about being spanked—to be humiliated in front of the others.*

Diane finished her dessert, realizing she was aroused . She had never been spanked in her life before, though she had privately read stories where a female had been spanked and had found them erotic.

"Dessert is finished."

Diane looked up at Stewart and at the females sitting next to him. They were watching her with undisguised interest, and one of the twin blondes had allowed or adjusted her cloth straps to uncover her breasts, as she looked at Diane.

Stewart leaned back in his chair, looking pleased. "I do believe the Ambassador has need to remind you of something."

LeBlanc cleared his throat. "I think everyone here is wondering if you are going to keep your agreement or break it because it's not to your liking."

"I keep my promises."

LeBlanc stood and walked over to her. "Please rise and bend over your chair."

Diane gave a small nod, her breathing was rapid as she slowly stood and leaned over on the arm of her chair.

LeBlanc took her leash and pulled her head down a bit more before wrapping the loose chain around the chair arm. "The spanking is normally done on bare skin of course."

Diane felt him undo a series of buttons along the side of her dress until he reached her waist and lifted the hem of her dress over the small of her back.

He kept his voice low. "Relax, if you can. I will be as gentle as I can."

The first few slaps were light, but then began to increase in force. Diane resisted flinching and crying out, clenching her jaw, as she stared down towards the floor. The spanking suddenly stopped with LeBlanc gently touching her cheeks. Her ass felt warm from the spanking, and she felt her nipples push against their jewellery.

LeBlanc undid her leash from the arm of the chair and she slowly stood straight. "You may sit now."

"Yes, Ambassador LeBlanc." Diane kept her voice low as she sat. She assumed she couldn't redo the buttons on the side of her dress yet. As she sat, she lifted up the hem and sat down on her bare ass. She knew she had to be wet, and hoped there wouldn't be a wet spot left on the chair. She looked directly at Stewart.

"Are you pleased now? Will that suffice to get you to ask the Minister of Defence to speak with the Charter of Conduct Office?"

He laughed. "I am more than pleased. I hope the Ambassador here will continue with your discipline and teaching later this evening."

Diane blushed. "I am not in need of discipline."

"So you claim. Was that your first spanking on Praxton?"

"I had never been spanked before."

He grinned at her. "Well, I can almost guarantee it won't be your last."

Diane took a drink from her wine and averted her eyes from his, wondering how he could be certain.

LeBlanc interrupted the conversation. "Shall we enjoy some refreshments outside? We have a lovely patio."

The table emptied as soon as Stewart agreed.

"Diane, would just check on Carol before we go, and make sure she's alright? Someone will come to release her very soon."

"Of course, Ambassador."

Diane walked over to Carol and asked her how she was doing.

"I'm fine. Actually a little bored, no one has touched me since dinner began."

Diane rested a hand on her chest. "I guess someone will be coming to let you go soon."

"The end of my big adventure..." She gave a grin. "I heard you getting a spanking."

"I did, by the Ambassador."

"Diane?" The ambassador spoke softly.

"Yes?"

"Are you alright? I will understand if you're upset with the spanking."

"I'm fine, really. Thank you for asking."

"Ah, good. I was concerned you might be a bit traumatized."

"Traumatized? No, I actually liked the experience in a way." She held the end of her leash out to LeBlanc. "I guess I need an escort to go outside."

"You do." He led her out of the dining room, and noticed the change in her posture and face as they walked. She looked calm, confident and poised compared to when he saw her before they arrived at the dining room.

The Ambassador walked a short distance with the Deputy Minister past the patio. He passed Diane's leash to Trina, who led her with the rest of the women to a table where refreshments were set up.

The twin blondes had both pushed their thin straps to the side. Unlike the other females, they left their breasts and nipples bare of any adornments. They pressed their bodies towards Diane as she reached for a drink.

"Hi, we think you're very pretty."

"Thank you." Diane felt one of the blondes rest a hand on her hip on the side where her dress was unbuttoned. "You two are very pretty too, but I'm really only into men."

"Maybe we can change your mind." One of the blondes pressed a nipple against her arm.

"Selena, Sylvia. Leave her alone."

The two blondes immediately walked away, leaving the senior female looking slightly amused.

"Sorry, they can be rather aggressive in their search for new playmates. My name is Trina."

"Diane. Thank you for your help."

"So, was that really your first spanking?"

"Yes it was."

"You did well. Most non-Praxton females would have been crying and jumping after each stroke."

"I was given some hints on how to act."

"Master Carl was talking about you before. He wasn't sure about you at all, and was worried how you would react."

"I guess he needn't be. He managed to get me spanked in front of everyone."

"But you took it like a Praxton female and made Ambassador Troy LeBlanc look good in the process by acting like he was your guardian. By wearing a leash, you showed you were open to Praxton customs."

"I understand it is important that Ambassador LeBlanc show that the Alliance Worlds are sensitive to Praxton customs."

"The Ambassador needs to look like he's in control before Master Carl will carry his message. You helped him immensely. I do hope war can be avoided."

"I as well."

Diane talked with Trina until LeBlanc returned. He took the end of the leash again, and an hour later said goodnight to the Deputy Minister and his females. Each of the females gave Diane a hug and a kiss, with the twins, in turn, lingering their kiss on her lips as they pressed their bodies against her. Trina gave her a quick kiss on her lips and then lifted Diane's skirt at the back to give her a quick slap on her ass. That reminded Diane how open the side of her dress was, and that it was the most provocative dress she had ever worn, even before the side buttons were undone.

The Deputy Minister inclined his head towards her. "Well, Diane, I know we disagree on a lot of things politically. You are also my adversary as well, being an Alliance citizen and a representative of the Charter of Conduct Office. But you have proven yourself to me tonight. You adopted Praxton customs and allowed yourself to be publicly spanked all to assist negotiations between our governments. You have my admiration."

"Thank you Deputy Minister Stewart. I hope our two sides can move closer together."

* * * *

"Well, that was a successful evening." LeBlanc kept hold of her leash and took her to a small patio table. He drew out a chair away from the table for her to sit down, her knees just reaching the table edge. Diane also flipped up her skirt at the back, letting it drape behind her. LeBlanc then hooked the end of the leash to back of her chair and sat next to her.

"I hope it was. May I take off these shoes? I'm not used to such a high heels and they're making my feet sore."

"Of, course." He watched her lean forward, exposing her side completely. The front of the dress fell between her legs, providing a small amount of modesty.

She sat up again. "That feels better." She pulled her dress back into place, aware he still could see a lot of bare skin. "I assume I require your permission to do up my dress."

"On Praxton you do."

She nodded. "And so far the permission has not been forthcoming." She twisted the wine glass in her hand. "I think I consumed a bit too much wine this evening and feel a little light headed."

"Praxton wine may be a little stronger than you are used to."

"I think you like the thought that strong wine gets me to imagine things. Last time we were here on the patio, you talked about using a napkin as a gag. Then I recall something about stripping me and taking me to the discipline room."

"It was only a flight of fantasy as I recall." He took a drink.

"I'm getting a bit annoyed with you."

"How?"

"You keep teasing me. Your flight of fancy last time, kept me from sleeping. Tonight you send me this dress that exposes me even if it's done up. You have a naked Carol blindfolded, and tell me I should be touching her to make her feel better. I was already aroused at that point and you knew it. Then you spank me, bare assed, in front of everyone. Now you're sitting calmly, drinking wine, knowing full well how I'm feeling."

"I don't presume to know how you are feeling Diane." He refilled her glass.

"I don't believe that."

"Really...?"

"Am I risking another spanking by saying that?"

"You would be as a Praxton female."

"Look what I'm wearing." She held up her hands. "Collar, cuffs and a leash. They're locked and you have both the keys. How much more of a Praxton female do I have to be? Can I give you flight of fancy?"

"Of course."

"I heard that guardians will chain the female to their bed to establish control. I'm wondering if these cuffs are just decoration or if you actually plan on using them as they were intended. So, my flight of fancy is you leading me to your suite and then establishing your dominance over me." She looked away from him and quickly took a drink of her wine.

"Diane."

"Yes?" She studied the table as she ran her fingers down the length of her leash.

"Look at me."

She turned her head slowly.

"I had to wait until I was sure of your adjustment to the Praxton culture. Understand a man in my position cannot just force his will on females, especially ones that are of the Charter of Conduct Office. If we go to my suite tonight, I will use you for my own satisfaction."

"I know. I want to know what it's like. Do you want me to go to my

103

knees now and prove it?"

"No, that isn't necessary yet."

He stood and then walked behind her, his hands on her shoulders. "I think I will deal with any resistance first." He lowered his hands on her arms and pulled them behind her back.

Diane heard the click as the cuffs were joined together.

"Oh, that feels different," she whispered out of a hot breath.

"Stand."

He led her by the leash towards the elevator.

"You like the feeling of being controlled?"

"Right now I do," she admitted.

"Good, because now I shall take you to my suite."

Diane followed him into the elevator. Her nipples were burning as they swelled against the jewellery rings.

"I'm going to treat you like a disobedient Praxton female tonight. You will be spanked and secured to my bed."

Diane nodded. "Yes, Ambassador. I need to be shown that you are in control of me."

She felt like she was already on the edge of coming, and knew he could see it in her body. She began to hope that someone would see her being led by LeBlanc, vulnerable and unable to resist him.

The elevator doors opened, and he smacked her on her ass before he tugged on her leash.

Diane saw a female coming towards her along the hallway, recognizing her as one of the office staff. She looked surprised as they passed along the hallway, giving Diane a curious look after she acknowledged the ambassador. Diane kept her head straight as her body was surveyed.

LeBlanc's suite was quite large, consisting of several rooms. As he led her past the living room to the bedroom, she saw several framed pictures of females in restraints hung on the walls, some of them appearing to look happy, while others looking distressed.

He undid the rest of the buttons on her dress, leaving her naked in front of the bed. "On your stomach and then lift your ass. You need to be spanked."

Diane slid onto the bed and then lifted her hips.

LeBlanc waited a half minute as he surveyed her before giving her a hard spanking, not stopping until she began to kick her feet and cried out. "Ouch. That really stings."

"Did that feel good?"

"Hmm... I think I needed that." She rolled on her side and watched him as he undressed. She stared at his erection, wondering when he would decide to allow her to take it into her mouth.

He slid into the bed and she wiggled around until she managed to get her head on his shoulder.

"Aren't you going to take me now?"

"No, I want you to feel frustrated a bit longer. I want you to hunger for more and know I'm in control."

"I know you're in control and I can also see you need relief as well. Are you going make me kneel in front of you?"

"No, that will have to wait for when you officially submit to me after time in the discipline room. But you are right, I do need relief. On your back and slide away from the head of the bed."

Diane slid down, breathing deeply as LeBlanc straddled her. With his hands, he pressed her breasts together around his erection and began to slide up and down. He began to pump faster and suddenly she felt hot fluid spill out under her chin and down her chest.

He moaned and gasped for air as he rolled off her.

Diane closed her eyes, not wanting to move. "Is that what guardians usually do to their females?"

"No, but I choose to do so now to you, an Alliance female. If you do decide to have me as your guardian, then I will treat you like a Praxton female."

"Okay. What if I ask for you to be my guardian?" She looked down at her body, wet from his explosion. She felt even more aroused that he used her that way and wished he would allow her relief as well.

"Sit up and I'll release your cuffs so you may clean up."

She got up from the bed and before heading to the bathroom, turned to face him as her hand rubbed her wet breasts. "I did rather enjoy it when you used me."

When she returned to the bed, he cuffed her wrists behind her back again.

"You may then have to decide to resign from the Charter of Conduct Office."

"I know. I'm prepared to do that." Diane felt the wine taking over her thoughts and closed her eyes, falling asleep as she curled up against him.

* * * *

She woke up and saw LeBlanc getting dressed. "You're leaving?"

"In a few minutes. I suggest you make use of the bathroom now, because I'm going to use restraints on you to keep you in the bed."

"But I have work, reports to do."

"You have two minutes. Better get moving to the bathroom."

Diane rolled out of bed and went to the bathroom. "This isn't fair."

He didn't say anything until she returned to the bedroom. "On your knees."

She looked at him and then dropped to her knees. He stepped towards her and pulled her face into his crotch, holding it there.

She felt the outline of his cock as it began to stiffen.

"I am going to be your guardian. What you feel against your face right now is all that is important to you. Understand?"

She tried to nod. "Hmm..."

"You have some learning to do, discipline is required. Do you agree?"

Again, she tried to speak, ending up muffling her answer as she nodded.

Diane felt his cock move upward and tried to press her lips against it through his pants to let him know she was surrendering.

"Good. Now get back into bed. I will deal with you later."

Diane reluctantly pulled her head away from his crotch, stood, and went back to bed. She watched as LeBlanc locked her ankle cuff to the bed.

"Now you will stay there until I decide otherwise. I will be having your suite closed to you. Only I or Carol Miller will have access. I will also be taking you to the discipline room downstairs later. Of course, if you tell me right now you don't want me as your guardian and wish to be treated only as an Alliance female, I will let you go."

Diane hesitated a few seconds before answering. "No Master Troy, I want to have you as my guardian."

"Good, I'll send Carol to check on you later."

Chapter Nine

Terri took a sip of her drink as she listened to one of the Steelet females describe how they were going to perform the show. She sat with the Steelets at a simple table with chairs at one end of the stage as they waited for Black Steel and the camera crew.

"So we are all going to get new outfits. New black skirts and the tops that are steel grey in colour. Terri, your outfit is going to be a white skirt with the steel grey top. The original show used four females, but we have modified it to use four Steelet girls and Terri."

Terri looked around the empty stage. Soon the holographic projectors would transform the stage to a roomful of dancing people in a nightclub. Black Steel would do his stage show, dancing and singing to the largely imaginary crowd, though there would be also real actors.

She finally saw Ed Roslyn, who used the stage name of Black Steel, enter from the far end of the stage and watched him approach. He wasn't what she expected when she first met him, not projecting the bad boy image that made him famous. Unlike his stage character, Ed Roslyn was quiet spoken and didn't exhibit a lot of energy. He took his entertainment business seriously and had made Black Steel successful financially.

"Okay ladies. I guess we'll review what we're going to do first, and then you can change into your new outfits." Roslyn stood at the front of the table with the five females looking up at him.

"First, besides the skirts and tops, I have also decided to have you wear new collars, cuffs and chains. These new collars and cuffs are made out of real metal and are fairly thick, so you will notice a bit of weight to them. I believe this will make our video more realistic. Terri, your collar and cuffs will be white metal, while the others will have black steel. This will provide more of a contrast between the Steelets and Terri. That is something the producer has indicated will make the video more successful."

Roslyn turned his attention to Terri. "When you performed on stage at the Crystal Ceiling during my show, I used a foam whip that left paint on your body. Romie and I have discussed the video at length and we have decided to make the whipping a little more authentic. The whip will still be made out of foam, but will be of much denser material, so it will look much more like a real whip. It will still leave coloured paint on your body, but it will also sting a little. Romie assured me you will be able to handle it and that if you feel the whip, you will react better on the video."

Terri nodded. "I'm not used to being on stage so maybe a more realistic whipping probably will help me act better. It won't hurt much will it?"

"No, just a bit of stinging. Now unless there are any more questions, I suggest we get ready for a few publicity shots and the video."

Terri changed into her new costume. Her panties consisted of a small triangular patch of white cloth with strings holding it into place. Her white skirt was short and tight, and the grey top was a form-fitting bodice that zipped up at the back. She strapped on her white stilettos and then put on the matching collar and cuffs. The collar was two inches wide and was locked with a padlock at the front. Four rings were mounted around the collar and she used two of them to attach chains that ran to her wrist cuffs.

She looked at the Steelets who were wearing outfits identical to hers, except for the colour. The Steelets also wore a pair of black nipple clamps attached with a small chain. Terri would have liked to wear a set herself, but Black Steel told her it might interfere with the whip and he wanted her nipples to be clearly visible. She was going to be a star in the video, and he needed her body to be bared as much as possible. Terri suspected the Steelets were a bit jealous she had taken over from them in the redone *Strike Her!* video, but they acted professionally towards her.

She finished dressing and then went with the Steelets for the photo shoot. They took several photos of the five females clustered around Black Steel. They changed position of the females with Terri usually in front. A couple of pictures were also taken with all the females topless.

* * * *

Terri concentrated on her dance steps while maintaining a smile as she moved through the holographic mall with the Steelets. She flirted with other mall patrons and sales clerks as she and the Steelets carried their purchases down the mall. It was another retake and she hoped she could make it look good this time. The Steelets showed that they were professional dancers and easily picked up the dance steps, making the moves effortlessly.

This time the director indicated he was pleased with most of the scene and called a break as he studied what had been shot so far.

Terri took a long drink of water and sat down at a table. One of the Steelets came over to her and sat down across from her. "You did pretty well back there. For someone without any dance experience, you picked up the steps really well."

"Thanks. I felt really awkward compared to the rest of you."

"Don't be. We've studied dance for years. Just wanted you to know we'll help you if we can."

The scene *Caught in the Act* was finally completed and they took a break while a new holographic image was set up with new props.

The next scene introduced Black Steel discovering how much Terri and the Steelets had spent while shopping, and the problems they had caused there.

He was dressed much like she had seen him before the last time he was on stage performing, wearing an open black vest and black pants. The pants were different this time in that a dark mesh several inches wide ran from the top of the pants to the crotch. He was obviously well endowed and whether it was natural or helped with the use of pills didn't matter to Terri. She took a long look at the partially visible cock.

Black Steel admonished them for their behaviour when they arrived home. Terri danced with the Steelets as he talked to them. Once again, Terri found it difficult to keep up with all the moves. One of the Steelets tried standing behind her and placing her hands on Terri's hips to show her how to move them. Several retakes and much laughter later, they managed to finish the middle part of the video called *Consequences*.

The final part of the video carried the title *Strike Her!* as well was the longest part, and while there was less dancing involved Terri was nervous about the rest of the action.

The dancing had the Steelets moving around Terri. First, the Steelets removed their tops and then their skirts as they circled around Terri. She admired how well they moved as they danced in their thong panties with the nipple clamps and chains glittering under the lights. The Steelets then turned their attention on Terri and began to undress her. Terri followed the script of trying to resist them, but was soon stripped of all her clothing.

Terri was led protesting to a chain and hook hanging from the ceiling. Her wrist cuffs were joined together and hung from the hook. There she waited with the Steelets dancing around her as Black Steel approached with a whip in his hand.

Black Steel lashed at her body, leaving a thin trail of different coloured paint after each stroke. Terri felt a sharp pain from each strike of the whip and soon was flinching as soon as Black Steel raised his arm with the whip.

Terri noticed Black Steel was starting to get an erection as he whipped her. She was getting aroused herself, knowing her nipples were erect and engorged. Where the whip had struck, her skin felt sensitive and alive. She hung from the cuffs as the script called on her to do, but she didn't have any trouble making it look realistic. She gasped for breath as her knees bent. When the whip struck her ass near the end, she let out a long moan.

"Again," Terri whispered.

Black Steel obliged and whipped her ass twice more. Then he undid her wrist cuffs and she fell to the floor, holding herself up by her arms. Black Steel threw away his whip and grabbed her collar, lifting her up. Terri's arms hung to her side as he pulled her against him.

She wondered briefly what Romie thought as he watched her, wondering if he was jealous. Terri felt Black Steel's member press against her through his mesh front, and then his hand cupped her breast. She tilted her head back at that cue, and he kissed her throat. Terri couldn't resist letting out a small moan. The script called for Black Steel to just hold her at that point with a camera fade out. But she heard the director yell more commands.

"It looks hot, continue, and don't stop!"

Black Steel squeezed her breast and his other hand moved from her collar to circle around her waist. Terri leaned back and placed one hand behind his neck for support as he bent down to kiss her other breast.

Terri opened her mouth to gulp in air. She was no longer acting, feeling aroused and under his control as he kissed her nipple. She wanted to drop to her knees and take his cock into her mouth, but instead closed her eyes and enjoyed his touch. Terri felt his hand behind her back slide up and pull her towards him and then his mouth was on hers. She enjoyed his tongue probing inside her and pushed her own tongue back.

When they broke off their kiss, Terri whispered, "Why don't you lay me down?"

He slowly eased her to the floor where she placed her hands above her head and arched her back. He dropped to his knees, straddled her waist and reached forward with his hands.

Terri let out a moan as his hands slid up from her rib cage and over her breasts and continued to her wrists, pinning her hands. He leaned forward and she looked at his erection through the mesh in his pants.

The director yelled, "Cut!" and Terri let out a sigh.

Black Steel looked at her. "Too bad it ended so soon."

"Maybe it's a good thing it did."

Black Steel stood and helped her up and she immediately looked towards Romie who was sitting with a few of the other of the spectators. He was watching her as she walked toward him.

Terri dropped to her knees and kept her legs parted a bit wider than Praxton protocol called for. She kept her head down and focused on his crotch. "I hope I didn't displease you during the show, Master Romie."

He lifted her chin up and she looked at his eyes.

"You did fine. It was a wonderful job of...acting." He gave her a grin. "Now go back to the others, it looks like they want to do a few photos."

* * * *

Terri was relieved. It seemed he had understood exactly what had happened and wasn't angry with her. She joined the others for the shot after the video, a picture along with the first that would be used as publicity for the video.

Black Steel stood with his back to the camera with the whip hanging from his hand. Facing him were the Steelets and Terri. The Steelets wore only their black thong panties, nipple clamps, and their collars and cuffs. Terri was nude, other than her collar and cuffs, and stood between a pair of Steelets on either side. Each female held a chain attached to a wrist or ankle cuff, pulling her arms and legs apart. They also photographed with Terri's back towards the camera and finally a shot of Terri lying on her back in front of the Steelets clustered together, this time naked.

Terri went with the rest to the dressing room. As soon as they entered, they let out a big cheer. Black Steel was the first to give her a hug and a kiss, followed by each Steelet female, who besides a passionate kiss, also gave her bum a few pats.

She reluctantly handed back her collar and cuffs and went into the dressing room shower. The water easily washed off the coloured paint from Terri's body, but a few marks from the whip remained, especially across her breasts and ass. She hit the dryer button. As she relaxed under the warm dry air, she noticed how her nipples stayed erect and her pussy lips were still swollen. *How am I going to make it through this day? I hope Master Romie takes me as soon as we get home.*

She stepped out of the shower stall and saw all the Steelets and Black Steel were waiting for her. Black Steel was now wearing his street clothes, but the Steelets were wearing their new uniforms and restraints. One Steelet stepped forward.

"We want to make you an honorary Steelet. So we want you to wear the Steelet uniform, yours to keep. We may need you in the future for other videos and performances."

Terri grinned and held back an urge to scream with excitement. "Thank you, thank you, thank you. This means so much to me."

The females helped her put on the collar and cuffs, nipple clamps and then her top and skirt. She looked in a viewscreen and grinned happily. One of Steelets attached the chains from all of her cuffs to the rings on her collar.

"There, you look like a proper captive now."

Black Steel then hooked a leash onto each of the Steelets, including Terri. He led them out of the dressing room to the cheers of the video crew, extras and spectators. Black Steel walked over to Romie and handed him her leash and the key to the locks.

"Thank you for allowing us to use her in the video. She did extremely well."

"You're welcome and I'm pleased to hear that."

"In an hour we're all meeting, the cast and crew, at Mermaids to review the video. Please join us," Black Steel invited.

"We'll be there. I would guess it will be rather quiet with the tourists gone."

"True, but we can have a few drinks to celebrate anyway. And maybe I can bribe the manager to allow us to use their nets."

Terri looked at Romie. She remembered Mermaids as the first nightclub they went to and how the club was known for capturing the women, sometimes naked, in nets located around the dance floor.

Romie answered, "We'll be glad to attend."

* * * *

Romie took Terri to dinner at a small family run restaurant in the mall. Like all the businesses in the tourist mall, it was quiet and desperately needing customers. The manager complained that if the tourists stayed away, he would have to lay off his staff, and they were all family.

"I would never hear the end of it if I were to lay off my brother and sister," he said with a grin.

After he went away Terri commented, "It must be tough for them, all these places that depend on tourists."

"It is. But I heard that the Praxton government is subsidizing the businesses here."

"Good. The manager seemed like a nice man."

"Speaking of nice that was quite the video you did there."

Terri felt her face redden. "I didn't mean for it to go so far."

"But you did enjoy being stripped of your clothes and whipped."

"I did. I don't why, but I got very aroused by it." She took a bite of her food. "It's not just the whip I liked so much, but rather I was naked and in restraints. Then this powerful man is holding this whip, who would decide how much punishment I would receive and there's nothing I can do about it. I'm exposed to whatever he wants to do, and my body can't hide that it wants him to continue."

"So what would've happened if the director hadn't called cut?"

Terri looked down at her plate and replied in a quiet voice. "I'm ashamed to say I was no longer strong enough to refuse whatever he wanted." She thought of Black Steel's erection and knew how much she wanted to have it inside her.

"That's okay. Males have power over females on Praxton and are expected to show restraint. Once a female is wearing a collar and cuffs, she often will be submissive to most males. It is easy then for males to take advantage of her. It is not your fault you felt weak and aroused. It is a perfectly natural feeling."

Terri smiled. "I want you to know my perfectly natural arousal is still with me."

"That is good to know and I will take advantage of that. It's also good to know that you enjoyed the touch of the whip. The discipline room hasn't been used for a while." He took the end of her leash. "Come. Let's go to the nightclub now."

Terri was led by a leash by Romie as they entered Mermaids. He didn't comment much more after dinner on her interaction with Black Steel, other than indicate she was looking flushed after her performance. He did praise her, telling her she worked the camera very well and the video should be interesting to see.

Mermaid's was quiet compared to last time she was there, and the lack of tourists had caused many of the nightclubs to shut their doors at least until the hostilities were over. The lights and special effects were working as normal, and with the music playing, the Black Steel crew were soon having a good time.

Terri sat next to the Steelets after Romie unlatched the leash from her collar and chatted with them about how much fun she had making the video. She was still feeling aroused from her performance, and after a couple of drinks, asked Romie if she could remove her top after the rest of the Steelets had done so. He quickly gave her permission.

Mermaid's decor included several huge aquariums along the walls that contained holographic images of fish and other sea creatures. On the clear glass floor mermaids, mermen, fish and the occasional sea monster swam underneath. The ceiling looked like they were looking up at the bottom of an ocean surface with green ripples dancing above them. Terri looked toward the dance floor and remembered the reason oversized fish nets were hung around the sides. They were used to hold the laughing and undressed female customers at special times announced by the bar manager.

Soon after they had a few drinks, the bar manager announced they were ready to show the video that was going to be sent to the Alliance worlds. Everyone turned their attention to the partial holographic video shown on the large screens.

The first part of the video was the simulated mall with Praxton citizens moving about and purchasing goods. A fashion show was presented, showing female and male fashions, including various clothing as well as the collar, cuffs and chains that had made Praxton famous.

The fashion was replaced by scenes in a nightclub showing people drinking, dancing, singing and a healthy dose of female nudity. The women were shown taking off their tops, and occasionally skirts, to dance under the flashing coloured lights. From the nightclub, the video changed to music of Black Steel.

The trio of songs that comprised *Strike Her!* were redone for the video from what was normally played by Black Steel. More mixing with additional musicians made each song sound richer than Terri remembered.

Terri saw how the camera stayed close to her body so the problem of her missed dance steps wasn't easily noticed. The Steelets also moved around her, making any mistakes hard to see. In the second part of the song, when she was stripped by the Steelets, the camera circled them as they performed, again making it hard to notice if Terri missed a move or a step. The final song concentrated on Terri quickly moving from where the whip was striking her, to her face, and then to another part of her body.

Terri bit her lower lip as she watched herself perform. She was naked and obviously very aroused during her discipline. The camera did close-ups of her breasts with her nipples erect as the whip struck them. When the video ended with Black Steel kneeling over her, everyone in the room cheered and applauded as Terri blushed. She remembered she was close to climaxing during the video, and it seemed everyone in the room could see that as well.

She turned to Romie, glad he wasn't angry with her being so aroused by Black Steel.

He touched her hand. "I know what was happening. You did wonderful there. I know it wasn't just acting. How could it be? You are a woman and were responding to the stimuli around and on you. You exposed your body and soul to help make this video. If it helps Praxton even in a small way, I hope you'll understand it was worth it."

"Thank you, Master Romie. Is this the completed video I'm to send to Mila?"

He nodded. "I wish we had more time to add a bit more or refine it, but I think overall the message will be as good as we can get."

The music increased in volume and soon the Black Steel crew were dancing. Romie let Terri go and dance. He then sat back and watched her dance with the Steelets.

After Romie had another drink, he walked down to the dance floor and joined Terri. She was pleased he was there and focused her attention on him even as she danced with the Steelets around her. Terri guessed that it wasn't a coincidence he was there when on the next song the bar manager announced it was Mermaid Catch Time.

Predictably, several of the women squealed as the men herded them towards the nets being lowered on the floor. All the females quickly took off their shoes and some removed their clothing as well. Terri spotted Karen DuPont run to the dance floor with Gary close behind her. He was encouraging her to move faster by quick pats on her ass.

She stopped where Terri was waiting by an open net.

"Wait for me." Karen quickly tossed off her shoes, top and skirt. "This looks like fun."

Terri took off her skirt as well and grabbed Karen's hand. "It is. The first time the nets just hold us for a few minutes. The second time, all the females get naked, because they spray water on us while we're caught in the net. It's a riot of screaming, squirming females."

They climbed into the large rope netting and seconds later, they were lifted in the air. Bodies and limbs intertwined and Karen took advantage of being pressed against Terri to fondle and touch her. Terri had one arm dangling out of the netting and used the other arm to put around Karen's shoulder.

Karen did have both hands free and used one hand to cup Terri's breast and squeezed it gently as her other hand stroked her ass.

"You got me at a slight disadvantage."

"Just to let you know, I plan on asking Master Romie to have you stay over my place one weekend soon."

Terri looked into her eyes. "I guess if he agrees, that will be alright."

"I can be a little dominant, so be warned that I will try to keep you in locked chains."

Terri felt Karen press her thigh between her legs. "I need to think about that part." She kissed her on the lips. "See I'm kind of seeing this girl, Allison, and don't know if I should have relations with other females. I like you, but maybe more as a friend right now."

Karen gave her a quick kiss back. "That's fine. Friends for the time being then. Maybe I'll change your mind later on."

After the nets were lowered, Terri scooped up her shoes and skirt, and approached Romie.

"That was fun. Can I leave my skirt off and stay in my panties?"

He gave her a grin. "Why don't you take those off too? Soon they'll have the call for the wet mermaid catch anyway."

"Good, I like being naked and helpless around you, Master Romie." She took off her panties and walked with him to their table. "Karen was telling me she wants to have me stay over soon at her place."

"You want to do that? She can be aggressive."

"I know she can be. But I think it'll be okay. I told her I wanted to be friends for the time being and she agreed."

"You do understand you can have only one guardian, but can have more than one female partner if you wish?"

"I...I know about one guardian and I guess it makes sense I can have more than one female partner. But I always only had one partner, a male partner, at any time before. So, I find this concept of having a girlfriend and a guardian strange, let alone having multiple girlfriends."

"I think you've adjusted well so far." He put his arm around her waist and pulled her towards him, giving her a kiss.

As more drinks were consumed, more females began to remove more of their clothing.

Romie turned to her. "See the trend you started? All these females are taking off their clothes."

She looked around. "So they are. I like it when there're a bunch of females naked. That way I can be naked too without feeling out of place."

"You are devious." He reached over and squeezed her thigh.

"If you think I'm being bad, I would think that you would spank me."

He grinned. "Right here and now?"

"Here, so everyone can see you spank me."

Romie stood up and grabbed her arm. "Lean over on your chair."

"Yes, Master Romie." She leaned over her bar stool and reached behind her back and clasped her hands together. She saw a few amused people gather around to watch her being spanked.

Romie gave her a few light slaps on her ass. "Now spread your legs."

Terri complied and he spanked her harder, turning her cheeks pink. When he stopped, she turned around and sighed. "Thank you. I needed that."

A bell went off and the bar manager announced, "It's Mermaid time!"

There was sudden rush to the dance floor. The females took off what clothes they had left on and crowded into the nets. Karen once again joined up with Terri, and soon they were crushed together as the net was lifted up.

Terri found her face was in line with one of the Steelets breasts. Karen was behind Terri and one of her hands was squeezing Terri's breast. Terri moaned.

Karen licked at Terri's ear. "Feels good doesn't it?"

"It does." Terri leaned forward and kissed the breasts in front of her.

A voice just above her called out, "Hey, don't start something you can't finish."

"Sorry, just was too inviting." Terri then leaned forward again and put her mouth over her nipple, sucking on it briefly and then released it. "Sorry again..."

"I'd say you deserve a spanking, but you seem to like those too much."

The net shifted position causing a lot screams. That was followed by a spray of water from above and below. The screaming increased in intensity.

Someone's hand was squeezing Terri's breast and nipple. Terri determined it wasn't Karen as her back was now to her. The hand moved and began to play with her other breast and nipple.

"I don't know who's doing that but it feels good," Terri called out.

"Let's just say it's fair turn around."

Terri laughed, recognizing the voice.

The nets were lowered and the wet and laughing females slowly untangled themselves from each other and the net.

Karen and Terri got to their feet and walked naked with their arms around each other's waists, laughing as water dripped off them.

"I have heard about Mermaids, but never was inside before. There are some regulation about Praxton employees not going to entertainment places and unduly taking advantage of tourists. That was just so much fun."

"It was. I better get dressed and go and send that video to Mila. Celebrating time is over for now."

"Okay, I'll call you soon."

"Thanks. Master Romie said it'd be okay for us to get together."

Chapter Ten

Gallagher looked at his assignment and frowned. It was not what he was expecting. He had been chosen to escort civilians to safety. Something he thought should be given to a more junior officer.

"Something wrong, Lieutenant?"

Gallagher turned to look at Captain Conley. "I didn't expect to be escorting civilians, sir. I was under the impression my performance has been satisfactory."

"It is." The Captain frowned. "Sometimes it is difficult to reward good men. I know your career has been held back because you were not born on Praxton."

"This assignment is a reward then, sir?"

"It is, if you consider who the passengers are. I believe there is one female that you are on friendly terms with. This might be an opportunity for you to know her better. As far as seeing war time action, there will be plenty of time for that later."

Gallagher slowly nodded. "I see, sir. Thank you, sir."

"Quite alright. We'll see you in the battlefield soon enough. Enjoy your time with her."

The evening sky was clear as Gallagher stepped inside the transport vehicle. He received acknowledgment from the driver, Sergeant Doug Wilson, and turned his attention to the six women sitting in the back.

"I'm going to apologize in advance. This is a military vehicle and isn't designed for comfort. As you have heard, the Alliance worlds have given an ultimatum to the Praxton government, and because of the immediate threat, all aircraft are being used for military activities. Thus, we shall use this ground transport."

A female called out from the back. "At least it's better than walking."

Gallagher grinned. "Tell me that after the ride."

He sat in the back next to Nicole.

"I'm glad we got to spend a bit more time together."

"Me too. Maybe we can keep in touch afterwards. I hope this Alliance world thing blows over soon."

"I hope so."

"How's your knee?"

"It's okay, just a bit stiff."

"I feel a bit bad about that."

"Well, after I get my collar on you I think there might be a spanking waiting for you as well."

She looked at him and bit her lower lip. "Well, I guess I may deserve a small one."

The vehicle lurched forward, causing the women to slide back in their seats. A few minutes later, the transport vehicle bounced over the rough road across the desert. Gallagher looked out the viewscreen at the landscape and then up at the sky. The transport didn't have any windows that might make it more vulnerable to attack, and instead depended on viewscreens to give an image of the outside. So far, he didn't see any activity, but he knew when the Alliance military attacked the base, aircraft and any military vehicles would be targets. It was thought aircraft might be the first targets, and the base commander believed ground transportation would be the safest way to get any civilians off the base, besides having a shortage of aircraft as the military hurried to move troops and supplies.

Gallagher continued to check monitors and the viewscreens while chatting with Nicole.

"So, when are you going to have time to get me a collar? Am I supposed to just wait until this is all over?"

"I'll think of something, even if I have to make a collar with my bare hands."

"Oh, does that mean you have plans for me?"

"How does being naked with your hands tied behind your back sound?"

"Interesting..."

"With your wrists tied to your ankles so you would be in a kneeling position."

"Hmm...Getting more interesting. Am I blindfolded too?"

"Of course..."

"A gag...?"

"No, I need to have access to your mouth."

"Goodness, what else is going to happen to me?"

"Nipple clamps."

"Good, I like those."

"And a crotch rope..."

"Not too tight I hope."

"As tight as I feel is necessary."

"Well, if you can get your collar on me, I won't be able to refuse to do what you want. I never liked the crotch ropes before, but if you put it on me, I think I may enjoy it."

"Lieutenant Gallagher?"

"Damn." He gave her a grin and then pressed the intercom button, connecting to the front cockpit. "Yes, sergeant?"

"Scanning image sensors have picked up military aircraft approaching approximately four dot two kilometres away, approaching at one hundred and twelve metres per minute. Intercept time is thirty-seven minutes away. Check that, acceleration is increasing, arrival time now twenty-two minutes."

"Change course to desert point two, and increase our speed to maximum safe. There is a large hill located there. Stop at a point opposite to the approaching craft."

"Yes, sir."

"Hang on ladies, things are about to get very bumpy. Make sure your harnesses are on tight."

Nicole thought if the transport vehicle had any shock absorbers, they should be returned for being defective. She would have been thrown out of her seat if it wasn't for the harness holding her in. All the same, she knew there would be bruises from the straps over her shoulders. She looked at Gallagher and could see the worry in his face. She was close enough to the intercom to know about the approaching aircraft and knew you didn't have to have a military mind to know they were sitting ducks for an attack.

"Sergeant."

"Yes, sir."

I want our defensive weapons locked on to targets, but do not fire unless we are shot at first. Let's not give them an excuse to blow us up."

"Done, sir. Acknowledged on waiting for first attack, sir."

Gallagher heard the nervousness in his voice.

"It's just a precaution, Sergeant. I don't believe they are looking for ground vehicles and have not noticed us yet. I expect them to do a fly past."

"Yes, sir."

Gallagher turned to the civilians in the transport. "If there is an attack, and I don't expect one to occur, be prepared to leave the transport. There are two exits, at the front as well as at the rear. Don't panic, Alliance military will not fire on civilians."

The transport bounced over the rough desert road, jolting the passengers side to side, plus up and down. Occasionally, one of the female passengers cried out making everyone feel even tenser.

Fifteen minutes later, Gallagher again responded to an intercom message. "Sir, there has been additional activity above. Some of our aircraft have engaged the hostile craft"

"Was there an exchange of fire?"

"None visual yet, sir."

"Keep me informed and push this buggy hard. We need to get out of sight."

"Yes, sir. We are near the hill at desert point two and will be stopping in a few minutes."

If the ride was rough before, it now felt like the transport was on the verge of going out of control. It became difficult even to make sense of the images from the viewscreens as the picture jumped from the ground and then the sky. Gallagher looked at the passengers, who were now too frightened to even scream. Suddenly the transport lurched to a stop.

"Sir, hostile craft have neutralized the Praxton craft and have resumed their course. There appear to be four ships, sir."

"Same course as before?"

"Yes, sir. Wait, one of the craft has changed course to our direction.

Check that, four enemy craft are coming in our direction.

"How long to possible engagement with us.?"

"Four minutes, sir. Fortunately they're at a fairly high altitude and don't seem to moving too fast."

"They're likely still giving aircraft a priority and are looking for a target bigger than us. Resume our course then, there's no point in hiding. Continue present direction and then stop in three minutes. We will then abandon the vehicle, and have it resume course on auto pilot. Make the appropriate adjustments now. Make sure you take the remote control with you when you leave." Gallagher went to the first aid cabinet and took out a blanket, coloured silver on one side and black on the other. He turned to the six females. "If we are stopped by hostile forces, I want them to believe you were being taken against your will. Therefore, I will be cuffing your hands together at your front and running a chain between them. I also want you to take off your shoes. It'll be easier for you to run barefoot than in high heels."

Nicole slipped off her shoes. "Collared, barefoot, cuffed and chained. Are you sure you don't want us naked too?"

He looked at her smiling face and grinned back. "That would be for later."

The women struggled to remove their shoes as the transport bounced along. The ride had shifted them in their seats sideways, up and down, causing their clothes to be rearranged. Skirts had risen over their hips, and breasts had occasionally slipped out of their tops.

Three minutes later the transport came to a sudden stop.

"Out, everyone out now!" Gallagher shouted as he undid his harness.

Passengers and crew scrambled out of the transport, and twenty seconds later the vehicle lurched forward again. Gallagher quickly attached military cuffs to the wrists of the females that weren't wearing any and attached a long chain to them.

He then led the six females, and the driver away from the road upon the transport they had been traveling, and then across the desert to where he knew a residual suburb existed. Night had fallen, but he still could see well enough from scattered light off the clouds.

"Follow me. Sergeant Wilson will be guarding our rear. Don't panic.

If I'm going too fast let me know."

Two minutes later, four black aircraft moved past them, their low humming noise reaching them from an altitude of fifteen hundred meters. They ran perpendicular to the road, heading towards a small outcropping of hills. One of the women complained about a stone hurting her foot, but they didn't slow down. As soon as they reached the hill, Gallagher ordered everyone to huddle together as tight as possible, and then put the blanket with the silver side in over them.

"The silver should keep our thermal signature from leaking out. You might feel a little warm. Sergeant, use the remote and stop the transport."

They waited under the blanket.

Gallagher whispered, "They'll stop at the transport and discover it's empty. Then they'll look for any occupants that may have run off. I don't believe they'll waste much time looking for us, but they have a number of sensors to detect heat, noise and small movements. So we have to keep still under this blanket and not make a sound."

The minutes passed and they heard an explosion.

"That would be the transport. They would've destroyed it after finding it empty and not having a use for it."

A deep throbbing noise increased in level and then slowly faded. After it disappeared and another ten minutes passed, Gallagher announced it was safe to leave.

They started walking across the desert.

"I guess you're going to keep us cuffed and chained together?" one of the women asked Gallagher.

"Yes, hostile troops may still return. Also it's easier for me to keep track of you if I know you're all together."

"Well at least he hasn't gagged us." Another woman spoke.

"Not yet, but I can arrange that."

Nicole winced in pain when she stepped on a small stone. So far, the sand had been relatively easy to walk on. She didn't believe it was necessary for the females to be chained together, but she guessed Gallagher, like most males on Praxton, always wanted to believe he had control over the women.

The temperature had dropped from the daytime, and walking was pleasant. Nicole chose to wear a loose, short skirt and a top with an open wide V at the front and back that came to a point at the bottom. The problem, she noticed, was that the top had a tendency to slide off her shoulder. Occasionally, she tried pushing the fabric back up shoulder, but her hands were restricted from movement with the chains. She finally gave up on the struggle and let the top slide down her shoulder, first on one side and then the other. Her breasts became exposed as the top slid down, and she considered that eventually the top might fall down completely. She decided it was Gallagher's fault if it did for keeping her wrists shackled together and chained to the other females.

She noticed the female in front of her was wearing a tight, short, elastic fabric skirt that had gradually risen up as she walked. She had initially tugged down on the skirt, but eventually, like Nicole, gave up with the restrictions placed on her wrists and let the elastic material rise up to expose the bottom of her cheeks.

Gallagher went to each female and offered them a drink of water from a canteen as they walked. When he reached Nicole, she asked him how much longer they had to walk.

"About another hour should do it."

"Well, in about another ten minutes my top is going to fall down. I take it you're going to keep us chained together?"

"I think so. Need to be safe."

"So, I guess I'm going to show off my boobs."

"The female behind you has had one breast exposed for most of the walk from the same problem as you."

"I'm sure you enjoyed the sight."

"Not as much as seeing yours." He reached over and gave her top the slightest push down. Her breasts popped into view.

"Oh, thanks. Pick on a poor girl chained up."

"I would rather have you naked with my collar on you."

"If you have a jewelled collar handy, you can strip me, but you don't. So behave yourself."

"Jewelled?"

"I'm special. If you want to collar me, it better be special. Then you can do what you want with me, soldier."

"I thought you had agreed to any collar I could come up with."

"Well, I would take any collar from you, but I was thinking if you

127

want to tie me up and put a crotch rope on me, maybe I deserve a special collar."

He shook his head. "You don't make it easy." He walked up to the next female.

Nicole noted Gallagher hadn't refused the notion of buying her an expensive collar. Her feet were getting sore from walking on the sand and she hoped it wouldn't be much longer before they could stop. She looked down at her wrists at the chain that ran from them to the other females. She had become a freelancer because she didn't like the control a guardian could place on her. Now she found she was getting use to the restraints, and was amused how Gallagher had insisted on keeping the females chained together. There was some validity to his worries if Alliance troops found them, but she suspected it was more because he also liked having the six women in restraints.

It was less than an hour when the end of the desert was reached, and they found themselves first in a small park and then at the beginning of a residential suburb.

"Should I radio the base, sir?" The sergeant asked Gallagher.

"You can try, Sergeant. I am going to guess that the hostile forces have jammed radio communications."

Wilson tried the radio, but found only static. "I guess you were right there, Lieutenant."

"We will have to find another way to report to the base. Meanwhile I think we should undo the chains and restraints on the females now."

"Yes, sir."

Nicole walked over to Gallagher, slipping her top back into place. "So now what happens?"

He pursed his lips. "It's best that we find some accommodation for you and the other females. Then I can make my way back to the base with the sergeant."

"Don't you dare leave us alone here! As far as going back to the base, all that will do is get yourself killed."

Gallagher considered her words and slowly nodded. "You may be right there. I have to come up with a plan."

They walked past several homes, looking for one that appeared large enough to hold all of them. Gallagher led the way to the entrance gate and waited until the security system analysed them. The gate unlocked, and they walked to the front door.

They were greeted by a tall, athletic woman named Angela who introduced herself as the senior female of the house. Gallagher indicated they were in search of a place to stay and after a short discussion, they were invited in. Angela told them Master Alex would be home shortly to discuss their needs, but in the meantime, they could make themselves comfortable. She led them to a sitting room, and they were soon joined by four other females of the household. Angela asked one of the other females of the household to bring in refreshments and Cassandra, a strawberry blonde, immediately went to the kitchen.

Angela then focused on the guests, noticing the females were all without shoes and two of them were without collars. "May I ask what happened?"

"We were returning these females back from a military base when we were attacked by Alliance forces. We had to abandon the transport and walk the rest of the way. Unfortunately, they had to remove their shoes to walk across the desert. I'm sure their feet are pretty sore."

"I believe that. I noticed the lack of collars. Are they freelancers?"

Gallagher nodded. "Yes, they were used for some military exercises."

Angela frowned. "Perhaps they're pleased the Alliance forces have come to free everyone."

Nicole spoke up. "No, that isn't true. I want to wear a collar from Master Lloyd." She turned towards him.

Angela frowned at the information. "I hope for you that will happen. The news is grim so far."

A slim brunette spoke up. "My girlfriend Terri is working on something to help us. We haven't lost yet."

"What is she doing?"

"She has found a way to bypass the communication block to the Alliance worlds and is sending information that refutes the Charter of Conduct propaganda."

Gallagher leaned forward in his chair. "Well, then there are two things I wish to ask. Can I meet this Terri, and see how she managed to send this message? And do you know where I can get a collar for

Nicole?"

"I want a nice one, remember?" Nicole interjected.

Gallagher nodded. "Of course."

"Is it possible we could wash up?" Nicole pointed at her feet. "We're a bit dusty from the desert walk."

"Of course. Cristal, show them where they can wash up and take their clothes and have them cleaned."

Chapter Eleven

Lucinda Taylor sat with her harness holding her in her chair as she faced the interior of the ship. The circular vessel had been built specifically in case of an attack by the Alliance forces.

The pie shaped craft held ten personnel seated around the perimeter. The power plant was housed in a metal column in the center that gave the craft lift as well as the large power requirements needed to reduce inertia.

Praxton military recognized they weren't any match for the Alliance space craft, and instead devoted their energies to resistance along the ground. The ground and air mobility vehicle (GAAMV) was designed to fly at low altitudes close to the ground. It was highly manoeuvrable and could make rapid changes in its direction without affecting the passengers, due to reduction in inertia. The craft had a textured top to resemble the reddish, desert soil of Praxton, but also had sensors and dampeners that adjusted for radar and other image seeking beams used by enemy craft to detect its presence. Heat generated by the power supply was sent through an air conditioner first to remove any sign of the craft's engine.

Lucinda looked across the room and saw Corporal Eric Winston studying a notepad that held the details of their assignments. She wondered when they would have time together again and if he was going to collar her to have her submit to him. She had made up her mind that he could be her guardian after he had stripped her and then given her a hard spanking. Unfortunately, the emergency siren had interrupted them, and she was left wondering how serious he was about her.

She hoped that he had noticed her as they boarded the aircraft. She wore the female military short skirt and top with the high boots, though she made sure her skirt and top were definitely on the tight side. But, unlike most of the other females, she left off her panties and bra, remembering his preference that she not wear underwear. Her emotions were jumping from thinking about Eric to the fact they were on an actual military mission. She tried to keep her thoughts focused on what they had to do once the aircraft stopped. Viewscreens were mounted around the interior of the ship, but she found the rapidly changing scenes made her dizzy as the ship made quick turns close to the ground as it headed towards its destination.

An alarm bell sounded and the voice of the pilot announced, "Prepare for landing in five seconds."

In exactly five seconds, the ship landed with a jarring stop, and an exit door immediately opened.

Eric announced, "Attention! Deploy operation QUACK one."

Lucinda and the others quickly left their seats and hurried to the exit, and began to assemble the tripods on the desert surface. The tripods launched bullet shaped weapons almost eight inches long and four inches in diameter. The Quick Accelerating Controlled Kill (QUACK) devices continued to seek the original targets by using sensors and a laser target beam. The nose of the oversized bullet was adjusted to help keep it on course, causing it to fly in an erratic fashion that helped avoid being hit by defensive systems. As it reached its target, a second propellant accelerated the weapon, while a laser beam was emitted to heat the surface of the target to weaken it. When the weapon hit, it had both an extraordinary high speed and an explosive charge hitting a less the perfect surface.

Lucinda and others finished assembling the QUACK system and signalled Eric they were finished. He did a quick inspection and ordered them back on board. As Lucinda passed him, he gave her a smart slap on her ass. She turned and gave him a grin before entering the ship.

She saw that he was watching her as she sat down. She lifted her skirt slightly to show as much of her legs as possible and then tightened the seat harness. She gave him a shy smile, hoping he knew she wasn't wearing any panties.

The ship stopped several more times and the crew set up more tripods. When they received word the Alliance military space craft were entering the atmosphere and invading the strike zone of the QUACK system, they sent a signal to the tripods. Each tripod launched a QUACK every second and each held a supply of well over a hundred shells. The weapon was not expected to last long before the tripod was destroyed by counter measures of the target. Thus, several tripods were set up to make it difficult for the Alliance ships to take out all the QUACKS.

The Alliance ships were surprised by the lack of a challenge by Praxton military vessels and surprised again by the small QUACK weapons. Several of the large ships were damaged enough they had to leave Praxton airspace for repairs, while a few more crash landed on the surface. More than half of the ships managed to make it to the surface and begin a ground assault on Praxton military bases and equipment. It wasn't an easy task. Praxton military didn't want to fight the superior Alliance ships in the air, but were much more prepared for desert warfare.

* * * *

Diane fell asleep after the Ambassador left and then woke up alone, her ankle still cuffed to the bed. She tried to fall back asleep again, but her mind wouldn't let her.

An hour had passed when Carol entered the bedroom carrying a tray of tea and toast.

"Good morning. I hope you slept well."

"I did. But I have work to do, and Master Troy left me chained to this bed." Diane sat naked on the bed with her arms behind her back, the bed sheet at her knees.

"Well you'll have to get used to it. Master Troy did say you may go to the washroom, but otherwise you will spend the day in this bed."

"But I have reports to do."

"Not today."

"So, I have to stay in bed all day. Then what?"

"Later this afternoon I will help you prepare for him. You will be dining with him in the staff lounge."

"Maybe I'll still change my mind about him being my guardian." Diane shook her head.

"You're being bad you know," Carol stated.

"So?" Diane watched Carol place the tray on the bedside table.

"On your tummy." She pulled at Diane's shoulder.

Diane leaned forward and then fell face down on the bed.

"I'm going to give you a spanking."

"No! You can't do that."

"Yes I can, and if you resist I will make it harder."

Diane felt Carol's hand administer several smacks to her cheeks. "Ow! Carol's cheeks were still sore from last night. I'm not resisting, see?"

"Then no more talk of not having Master Troy as your guardian unless you really mean it?"

"I promise."

"Roll over."

Diane twisted around to her back.

Carol cupped one of Diane's breasts, bent down and kissed her nipple. "Hmm... I never had control over a female before. Kind of a neat feeling of power."

Diane suddenly felt aroused, or rather the arousal she had felt since last night came on stronger. She closed her eyes, trying to regain her composure. "What would Master Troy say about you doing this?"

"He would approve. Females are supposed to be close to each other." She bent down and sucked on Diane's other nipple and then returned to the first.

Diane arched her back and moaned.

"I can do whatever I want with you, can't I?"

"Yes, anything..."

Carol backed off the bed. "I think it's best we leave you in a state of frustration for Master Troy."

"That's cruel."

"Come on. I'm going to let you go to the washroom."

"Will you undo these wrists cuffs please?"

"Only for a little bit. You need to learn how it feels to be in restraints and get used to them."

Diane showered as Carol talked to her about the application to become a Praxton citizen and the build-up of military craft around Praxton. After she was finished, Carol handcuffed her wrists behind her back again.

"Back into the bed and on your stomach."

"Not another spanking?" Diane looked behind her as she rested on her stomach.

"No, just something I want to try on you." She attached ankle cuffs together and used a chain to link her ankles and wrists together, telling her, "Come on, reach back a little more."

"That's a little uncomfortable." Diane pulled her arms against the hogtie knot.

"You'll get used to it. It looks good for when Master Troy comes back. Roll on your side if you want to be more comfortable." She took another chain and attached it from her ankles to the foot of the bed.

Diane rolled to her side. She knew she was wet, her need for sex on display.

Carol brushed Diane's hair away from her face. "You look really sexy."

"Thanks. I feel helpless."

"Part of the sexy look."

Carol talked to her about Praxton, occasionally fixing her hair or running her fingertips over Diane's skin. Once, she played with Diane's nipples with her fingers until they were both erect. "You know, I do like this domination thing. I like it when Gordon makes me do what he wants and I like it when you're submissive to me. There's something arousing about a female in restraints, don't you think so?"

"You mean to both men and women?"

"Yeah. I like to look at viewscreen images of females in restraints, don't you?"

"I guess so. Do men on Praxton ever wear restraints?"

"Not in public. Social custom, females only. For a guy to wear cuffs or a collar, that would be like being a cross dresser here. I guess some guys might in private, but I've never seen it."

Carol slid onto the bed and placed Diane's head on her lap. "Is that more comfortable?"

"Yeah." She felt Carol's hand cup her breast and gently play with her nipple. "Carol? You're going to get me so horny I may come before Master Troy shows up."

Carol laughed. "Then I better stop. He'll be here soon."

LeBlanc came into the bedroom and saw Diane on her side with her head on Carol's lap. One of Carol's hands was tracing her fingertips on Diane's side.

"I see you two are getting along."

"Diane has been good, Master Troy."

"I'm pleased to hear that. Would you prepare her for dinner tonight in the lounge? She may go to her suite, but only for one hour to finish up some work." He spoke to Diane. "I will be taking you to the discipline room after dinner tonight. Be prepared."

He then left the room.

Carol looked at Diane. "Sounds like it's going to be quite a day for you coming up."

Diane was allowed to wear the white lace dress so she could go to her suite. After she put the dress on, her wrists were cuffed in front of her and her ankle cuffs were joined by a chain as well. Carol attached a leash to Diane's collar and led her to her suite with Diane taking quick short steps.

Diane protested one hour wasn't long enough, and with her wrists cuffed together, made work difficult, but Carol refused to relent.

"You have one hour with the cuffs on and that's it. Don't give me an excuse to give you another spanking."

Diane looked at her for a moment as she sat in front of the small desk. "Well, I wouldn't want for you to have any more fun that way." She continued to work and didn't resist when Carol attached the leash to her collar and pulled on it.

"Darn it, I am so behind in my work."

"Come on, I have to return you to Master Troy's suite."

"What about my stuff here, my clothes?"

"Off limits for the time being for you. You can only wear what Master Troy permits you."

Diane looked down at the white lace dress she was wearing. "He obviously doesn't want me to wear much. I'm barefoot and rather exposed under this dress."

"There is a new dress for you to wear for dinner. Plus a few accessories."

"A new dress? What does it look like?"

"It's short, I'll tell you that."

The dress was red, laced at the top and solid material from her waist down. It had short sleeves and reached only to mid-thigh. She was also given a pair of red thong panties to wear for modesty, because when she sat down, it was expected the dress would lift up. The dress also had a wide red belt with numerous rings around it. Carol cinched it tight and then locked it at the front.

"That's really tight."

"Small waist helps accent your boobs." Carol attached cuffs just above her elbows, her wrists and at her ankles. The cuffs were wide and each cuff was attached by a chain to her belt. Then Carol showed her the matching collar.

"I won't be able move my head."

"Sure you will, only a bit mind you."

"Great. Do I get shoes to wear with this?"

"I thought going barefoot would be okay, but then I found these red shoes that would look a lot better. Goes better with the look, I thought. What do you think?"

She looked at the stilettos with the open sides. "Barefoot comfort is out I guess. I'm just happy I get to wear panties."

"You will have to wait for Master Troy now. He should be around soon."

"Try to relax."

"In these shoes and dress...?"

"They do look good on you."

"Then I suppose it's all worth it."

Carol gave her a quick kiss and a pat on her ass before leaving Diane alone. Half an hour later, LeBlanc came in the room and surveyed her then nodded his approval. "You look wonderful."

"Thank you, Master Troy."

"You also look very sexy and vulnerable, and I can easily control you to do as I wish. How do you feel?"

Diane lowered her head. "I feel sexy and vulnerable to your wishes. Master Troy."

"Excellent. Shall we go then?"

LeBlanc led her into the dining room where Diane felt that everyone was watching her. It must seem quite a coup for LeBlanc, she thought, to transform a Charter of Conduct Office official into a Praxton female. But as she sat at a table, she felt content and relaxed. Diane felt captured and no longer in control. She knew LeBlanc was going to strip her and punish her, bend her to his will. He had taken away her means of communicating with the Alliance world. He had also taken away her clothes, making her wear what pleased him.

"How are you feeling now, Diane?"

She stared at him. "You have taken away everything from me, but I feel content." She looked around the room, thinking others in the room were whispering about her. Her dress gave more exposure than most of the Praxton fashions. Her dress lifted higher when she sat, revealing her legs to her hips, and the red lace of the dress showed the outline of her breasts under the lights of the dining room. She knew she wasn't allowed by Praxton customs to cross her legs nor keep them tightly together.

She carefully took a drink of her wine, her arm movement restricted by the wrist and elbow cuffs that were joined to her belt by chains.

"Are you looking forward to the rest of the evening?"

"It scares me a bit, the punishment. And then, when I must take you, which makes my stomach tighten up. But yes, I'm looking forward to it, Master Troy. When I first arrived here, I saw a video of this young woman, I think it was called *Strike Her!*,being held naked on stage at a nightclub. I found it erotic as she dangled from her wrists, being whipped and that she seemed to enjoy it. I've thought about that image several times, and I wondered what it would be like, to be tied up naked and whipped. As long as the whip didn't hurt too much, of course."

"Well you shall find out."

"Now I'm truly nervous."

He grinned. "Don't be. I will not harm you, but I will make your body feel alive."

"That doesn't sound so bad."

He whispered to her, "For your sake and mine I am keeping your submission to me confidential from outside the embassy. Carol Miller knows the truth of course, and most of the others here see you as my partner. They see you experimenting with the Praxton fashions as most women do when they visit the planet. I suspect they believe there may be more to our relationship. However, I have not used a leash on you, other than when Praxton guests have arrived, and therefore both of us are not breaking any rules openly."

"Eventually they will find out, Master Troy."

"Yes, this secret cannot last much longer. I hope to sustain it until after this current conflict is over. Then it may not matter."

Diane licked her lips. "I hope so."

After the meal, she waited until he came behind her and helped pull out her chair. When she stood, he undid the chains from her wrist cuffs and then joined the cuffs together behind her back. He then used one of the chains to attach her wrists to the back of the collar, lifting her wrists high on her back.

"I wanted to show these people that you and I are together. The collar and cuffs will show them you no longer have any resistance to me."

"I see. So cuffing my hands behind my back will do that?"

"I think so." He lifted up her dress and gave each cheek a smack. "With your arms pulled behind your back, it makes your breasts and nipples stand out more."

She looked down and saw her nipples and breasts were straining the lace fabric.

He led her past the other diners. Diane felt her face go red and knew her panties were now wet. When they left the dining room, he turned to her.

"I know how you must feel, but I felt it was necessary."

"Of course, Master Troy."

"Good, I will return you to my suite where Carol will help you prepare for this evening."

* * * *

"It's called a sub-dress, quite common on Praxton," Carol explained, "they're usually snug fitting like that, or of a sheer material. One side is usually open or made of a transparent material to show that the female is not wearing anything underneath. The dress always is under the arms without straps and with a single closure. That is so that when a female is in full restraints, the dress can still be easily removed." Carol had taken Diane back to LeBlanc's suite to get her ready for the last part of the evening.

Diane looked at herself in the mirror and nodded. "It does show everything." The thin white satin like material went from under her arms to just past her hips.

"Generally speaking, when you wear the sub dress, you don't wear nipple jewellery or a chastity belt either. Your body should be completely visible when the dress is off. The female is also normally barefoot as well."

"Then I guess I'm already dressed."

"Just a couple more details. First, he wants to me restrain your wrists behind your back."

Diane turned and put her wrists together behind her back. "Troy wants me rather helpless does he?"

"He does want you to feel that way. By the way, it is always Master Troy." She latched the wrists together.

"I'll remember that."

"When your guardian is present, and you are sitting or kneeling, you do not ever cross your legs. Keep your knees about a fist apart. When you are walking, standing and sitting, a female should be looking at her guardian's face, paying attention to his needs. When you are kneeling you look at his face when he speaks, but otherwise keep your eyes on his cock."

"Alright. Got that."

"He will discipline you. Resist crying out or flinching. Praxton women are strong and can take what punishment is handed out. The discipline will sting and hurt a bit, but it's against the law to damage the skin, so there are limits to what he can do. The custom on Praxton is when he feels he has completely dominated you and knows you will obey him, he will have you kneel in front of him. You then willingly take him in your mouth. The first time, the male nearly always goes off into the female's mouth."

"Oh, I never thought about that. I guess that symbolizes his domination and that he receives pleasure first."

"True, though when Gordon did it to me on our first time, I came as well. It's a pretty intense moment. It's more than sex. It's a commitment to each other in a way."

"I guess I can understand that better now."

"There is one more thing." Carol held up a round red ball with two straps attached to it.

"A gag?" Diane eyed the object. "I suppose he considers it a symbol as well." She thought about the napkin he gave her and after indicating it could be used as a gag.

Carol left it on the bed next to her. "He will likely have you wear it. Try to relax, Diane. He won't really hurt you, and you will enjoy the experience." She bent down and gave her a kiss. "Good luck. I'll check up on you later."

Diane waited for LeBlanc to show up. She stared at herself in the viewscreen, surprised on how in a few days she had accepted the role of a Praxton female and was looking forward to his domination over her. She felt erotic in her restraints.

LeBlanc entered after a single tap on the bedroom door. Diane sat up straight and watched him enter the room. He had changed from his ambassadorial formal clothes to a loose green shirt that was left open at the front. His pants were a dark grey and the fly consisted of a black mesh four inches wide with a zipper. His boots looked heavy and had thick soles that boosted his height. LeBlanc strode close to her and then gently brushed her hair from her eyes.

"Master Troy." Diane heard a slight quiver in her voice.

"Before we begin your introduction, I thought I'd better explain some things to you. Praxton was born out of conflict hundreds of years ago and to maintain peace certain customs were adopted. Like many traditions on Alliance worlds, the customs have been modified over time and sometimes it is hard to discern the reasons for them. Outsiders don't always understand another world's customs, and on Praxton that seems to definitely be the case.

"You are wearing a slave dress, now called a sub-dress, as the word slave has negative connotations. At one time, a female was either purchased at an auction or kidnapped. The master usually had several females and there was little point in obtaining the females if he couldn't trust them not to run away at every opportunity. The females in turn had to believe their master could control them and defend them. A master, who was too soft to punish his females, soon lost them. Therefore, it came to be that when a female was obtained through an auction or other means, he would feel it was an obligation to immediately show the females he had complete control and was able and willing to discipline her." LeBlanc paused as he inspected her wrists cuffed behind her back, and then stroked her arm with his fingertips.

"The slave dress was usually ripped off. This was to inspect her body, and to make her feel vulnerable to him. The dress was typically the colours and design of her previous owner, and so she would be issued one of his later. She was then gagged and led to a discipline area, usually with other females in attendance. There she was customarily whipped, although other methods were also occasionally deployed. After a period of time, her gag was removed and she would be asked if she had anything to say. Her first words were supposed to be, *I submit to you master.*

"She would be then allowed to kneel in front of him and take his cock into her mouth. He didn't always have ejaculate, because he might have half a dozen females to attend to that day. But once she took his cock, she was admitting he was her master."

"This ceremony happens to every female now on Praxton?"

"Oh no. In some cases the female and male spend time together first, sign contracts and then they would have a welcoming ceremony. Guests would arrive at the home and the female would wear a special dress that can be removed with a single pull at a knot. She is then revealed to all guests. Generally, she is also given gifts, as well as, a new collar from her master. It is also traditional for her to be disciplined in front of the guests."

"And in my case, you want to do a more traditional initiation."

"Yes. I think you will appreciate Praxton more this way." He held up the gag. "Are you ready?"

"I am." Her eyes focused on the red ball as he slowly moved it towards her mouth.

LeBlanc pushed the ball into her mouth and then secured the straps behind her head, fixing her hair out of the way. He then used the leash to lead her out of the room and down the hall to the elevators. He used his ID, ordering the elevator to go without stopping until they reached their destination. In the discipline room, they were alone when he stopped to speak to her.

"Don't be frightened. I won't hurt you. Perhaps some minor discomfort, that's all." He closed, but did not lock the door behind him.

She nodded.

"Now your dress."

"Umm..."

Leblanc undid the back of her dress by pulling a zipper down. The thin fabric collapsed under its own weight, leaving her naked.

He tugged at her leash, pulling her towards him.

"There, do you feel like you're completely under my control now? Full nipples. Makes me want to take advantage of them."

"Umm..."

"I want to punish you now. Do you want to feel what it is like to be punished?"

Diane closed her eyes and gave a slight nod. LeBlanc led her to a large X shaped cross object made of a dark material with several hooks at the top and bottom. He undid her wrist cuffs and pushed her flush against the cross. "Hands to the corners."

She raised her arms as high as she could reach. LeBlanc then latched her wrists to the cross. He pressed a button on the side and she heard a small motor pull her wrists up higher, until her feet left the floor.

LeBlanc pulled her legs to each side and latched her ankle cuffs. He went to the wall and picked up a multi-strand whip and showed it to her. "This won't hurt too much, just a bit of stinging."

She nodded and turned her head to the side so she could see him holding the whip. He walked out of her view. She felt the first strike on her back and he moved around, on her legs, sides, but largely on her ass.

"I want your cheeks nice and pink, a bit on the red side. That would be perfect I think."

Diane realized he was right. The whip didn't hurt so much, just leaving a mild stinging sensation. It also had the effect of increasing her arousal, and she knew she was getting wet. He stopped sooner than she expected.

"Nice and pink on your backside. Shall we do your front as well?" He stared at her face, waiting for a response.

She nodded quickly, "Uh hmm."

He reversed her on the cross, again pulling her arms up high, but this time forcing her legs even wider apart. "Very nice..." He lightly slapped at her breasts with the whip, and began to move up and down her body.

Diane tried not to show any emotion and flinched only when he grazed her pussy with the whip. Across the room, she saw Carol watching from the doorway. It was both humiliating and erotic to her that someone was watching her fall from an adversary to Praxton, to being the Ambassador's female. She knew she was no longer capable of representing the Charter of Conduct Office; she had become a rogue agent. It occurred to her the Ambassador had also gone too far in his appreciation of the Praxton culture, but might get away with it if he successfully helped bring Praxton under the Charter of Conduct.

"That is very good. I believe your whole body has that nice pink glow to it."

Diane looked down and saw her pink skin. She also saw how engorged her nipples were and knew she had to be dripping between her legs.

He pulled off her gag. "Do you have anything you wish to say?"

"Yes, I submit to you Master Troy."

He took her down from the cross and she immediately sank to her knees. She noticed her audience was still watching from the doorway.

"I shall restrain you as well. I want to make you feel totally submissive towards me."

"I do already."

"There is another level you shall reach." He attached her right wrist cuff to her left ankle cuff and repeated with her left wrist. Then he stood in front of her and opened his fly.

Diane watched his cock when it was pressing against the mesh of his fly, and then standing exposed in front of her face. She opened her mouth, and felt him rub its head around her lips, before slowly sliding it over her tongue.

"You will take all of it."

Diane resisted the gagging sensation as he pushed past her tongue and into her throat. She breathed deeply, inhaling his scent as he slid back and forth into her mouth. She sucked and worked her tongue around his cock, wanting him to go quickly as she struggled to get air into her lungs. She also felt like she was about to come herself, moving her hips forward and backward. Diane felt his hands tighten around her hair, pulling her head into him when he released into her mouth. She immediately sucked harder at his cock, swallowing the hot fluid as her own loins exploded in heat.

His cock was retreating in size, but he still kept it in her mouth, and she worked at him with her tongue as he pressed her head against his stomach.

Finally, he pulled out of her. Diane stayed on her knees and kept her eyes on his wet cock.

"You did well. I will now lead you to the cages."

She nodded as he undid her cuffs, but once again joined her wrists behind her back. She followed him to a cage where he placed her on the small bed, and then hooked her leash to the head of the bed.

"Have a rest here. I will come for you in an hour, Diane."

"Okay." She watched him lock the door, and walk slowly away.

Chapter Twelve

Nicole had made a sudden decision to announce she was willing to take Gallagher as a guardian by calling him Master Lloyd. It occurred to her, he was already acting like one to her as he led them across the desert, and if a war was going to happen, it would be nice to have him as a guardian. She wondered if he picked up the implication that she called him Master Lloyd, that she was not just being polite. Nicole hoped he was going to collar her soon, and now her demand for an expensive one earlier was not necessary.

All of the females gave their clothes to Cristal, and then used the communal shower room. The room held several open shower stalls plus a long counter for dressing and applying make-up. The rest of the females came up to her and immediately asked her about Lloyd becoming her guardian, and when he'd asked her.

"I hope it'll be soon." She laughed. "He said he wanted to collar me earlier last night, and now I think he would make a good guardian."

After showering, Nicole began brushing her hair when Lloyd entered the washroom. He was holding several items in his hand.

"Nicole, I have something for you. I borrowed them from Angela until I can buy proper ones myself."

Nicole looked at the collar, cuffs and chains hanging from his hand. "They…they look…wonderful." She fell to her knees as he approached, keeping her legs slightly parted as she looked up at him. She watched his hands slowly place the white metal collar around her neck and heard the small click as he locked it into place. She heard the other females around her murmur their approval, and had a glimpse of the several females standing at the entrance of the washroom watching.

"Your hands…"

Nicole raised her hands, and saw him place a cuff on each wrist slowly and carefully. He locked them and attached a short chain between them before latching a leash to her collar.

He placed his hand under her chin, lifted it and looked into her eyes. "Nicole, will you now accept me as your guardian?"

"Yes, Master Lloyd. I want nothing more."

"Excellent. Rise, it's time for dinner." He grinned as he lightly pulled on her leash.

Nicole sat next to Lloyd at the table, her leash attached to the back of her chair. The other females had received their clothes to wear again, but Lloyd had decided she was going to remain nude for at least the rest of the night. The table was big and could be made larger to hold the entire household, plus the guests, but the females of the household had eaten earlier, and only Angela and Master Alex joined them.

Alex told them that the Alliance forces had taken over the air space and some of the surface. So far, the Praxton forces had made the Alliance land assault difficult, but it would only be a matter of time before they would take over the planet.

Nicole listened intently to the conversation, worried about Praxton's fate. She was also feeling aroused as she looked down at her cuffed wrists and then at Lloyd, knowing she was now dependent on him for her safety. He also held the only keys to the locks on her collar and cuffs, enforcing his control over her.

After dinner, Lloyd led her to the outside patio, and after kissing her, told her she and the other females were invited to stay at the house as he tried to find a way to help his unit.

"I can't stay here, as much as I want to."

Nicole pouted. "I want you to stay here. If you leave maybe I can go with you."

He shook his head. "No, sorry. I'm going to have Angela in charge of you while I'm gone."

"I have to listen to her?"

"Yes, you do. I asked her to try to get you used to being in collar, cuffs and being undressed. She will also be in charge of your discipline."

Nicole looked like she was going protest and for a moment opened her mouth and then changed her mind. "If that's what you want, Master

Lloyd." She nodded. "Naked and in cuffs, it shall be then."

"I do. I also want to give you that spanking. I thought this would be a good place to do it, unless you prefer I spank you in front of the others."

"This would be a good place, Master Lloyd. But if you want to spank me in front of the others, that would be fine with me too."

"Well said." He pulled on her leash, leading her to a small bench on the patio and sat down.

Nicole leaned over his lap, placing her hands on the floor. She twisted her head back and watched his hand come down on her cheeks, alternating between them. She moaned and cried out softly as his hits became stronger. She knew Praxton women were not supposed to make unnecessary noises or complaints while they were being disciplined. In fact, it was a point of honour that Praxton females refused to admit to pain. Nicole was determined to follow the customs of Praxton now that she had accepted Lloyd as her guardian.

He stopped and massaged her cheeks. "I think you deserved that."

"I did."

"Then I guess it's time to go inside and see the others."

She continued to lie on his lap. "Master Lloyd, are you going to still spank me in front of the others? I think Praxton custom is for me to be disciplined in front of the others when you become my guardian."

"Good point."

She stood up and gave him a self-conscious smile. "Sorry for being forward about the spanking, but I want the other females to know that you are my guardian and capable of disciplining me."

He led her back into the house and to a recreation room where all the females were sitting around looking at a large holographic viewscreen. Some of the females were dressed, while others just wearing their panties as they crowded together on the chairs, couches and floor. They all called out to Nicole and offered congratulations as she blushed.

One of the females called out, "Do we get to see some discipline from the new guardian?"

Gallagher grinned. "Indeed you do." He led the now blushing Nicole to the couch, and sat between the females already sitting there. Nicole had to lie not only over his lap, but three other females as well. Gallagher started the spanking, and then a female sitting next to him took a couple of slaps as well. Several of the other females in the room then came over and added their hands on her ass as well.

Nicole let out a groan. "I don't think I deserve this much attention." She gasped and squeezed her fists. She held back from crying out loud deciding if Praxton females could be quiet during discipline, then she could as well. Still she felt one tear escape from her eye and her skin burning from the hits.

"Well, you needed the spanking."

Nicole slowly got up. "I know I did, but not from everyone." She grinned as the others laughed.

After they shared a drink with the group, Angela showed them to a guest room.

"I'm sure you will find it comfortable. There are additional restraints in the dresser drawer, if you want to make use of them."

"Thank you. Do you have enough beds for the other female guests?"

"Yes we do. Of course, the females will have to share beds. I assume you have no objection to them being cuffed to the beds for the night?"

Lloyd nodded. "Of course, as long as they are in your home, you have authority over them."

"Master Alex would like to talk you in private for a few minutes, if you don't mind."

Angela left and Lloyd turned to Nicole. "I'll be right back." He led her to a wall hook along the bedroom wall and lifted the chain between her cuffs over it. "Wait here."

Nicole looked up at her hands above her head. "I guess I don't have a choice."

He looked back at her, looking pleased. "You look good that way."

Nicole sighed as she waited. It was expected that a male show his dominance over a female once she accepted him as her guardian. So far, he had only kept her naked and in cuffs, plus the spanking. She was glad she suggested that he spank her in front of the others to prove he was in control of her, and that he was capable of disciplining her. She didn't expect all the females to join in the spanking, but it did mean they all liked her. He didn't spank her too hard, and Nicole believed he was showing restraint, because they were guests in Master Alex's home.

When Lloyd returned to the room, she expected he would exert his authority by spanking her harder and using a whip. Praxton customs dictated that if he didn't, she wouldn't respect him as much. A male who cannot discipline his females is considered weak, and Praxton females take pride they can absorb discipline without crying out. She had learned Lloyd wasn't born on Praxton like herself, but if they were to stay on Praxton, she wanted to follow their customs. Still she hoped that he wouldn't whip her hard.

The door opened to the bedroom and Nicole looked at Lloyd, trying to anticipate what he was going to do next.

* * * *

The GAAMV landed with a thud on the hard sandy surface, with smoke pouring out of the vents. Alarm bells rang as Eric called out instructions.

The inertia dampeners went offline during a last hit, and Lucinda felt the harness dig into her body. She then hit the harness release, tumbled out of her seat and raced to the exit, taking a rifle and a set of electronic goggles with her from the open box by the doorway.

She joined the others a short distance away from the downed craft, where there was an outcropping of rocks. Lucinda quickly checked her weapon and slipped on her goggles. Her breath came out in puffs as she rested on her stomach. She felt her heart pound in her chest as she examined the horizon in front of her, wondering what was going to happen next.

The GAAMV had survived two hits from the Alliance craft before a third hit tore open a vent tube and ruptured all navigation systems. Fortunately, no one was seriously hurt as the GAAMV spiralled four hundred feet down to the ground. After everyone had escaped from the ship, a self-destruct charge went off in the interior to destroy all vital electronics and information. Now the GAAMV team could only wait for either rescue or, more likely, enemy soldiers.

Lucinda tried to hold her gun steady as she watched Alliance spacecraft drop vehicles and soldiers to the desert and speed away. She watched the advancing army through her goggles that revolved them into individual forms. Information, such as speed and size, were shown on the eyepieces of the goggle. She could also change the parameters to read infrared, ultraviolet or any spectrum in between. All that information told her the Alliances forces were numerous and advancing quickly.

Explosions hit close to her, and she heard screams as the sand and rock fell around her. She tried to concentrate on firing her weapon. The battle lasted only a minute before they were overwhelmed by the Alliance soldiers, who first fired concussion bombs, and then flash grenades.

When Lucinda could see again, she was being placed in plastic handcuffs and dragged to a waiting transport. She twisted in the grip of the Alliance soldiers, only to see Eric lying on the ground with blood seeping out of a leg that was bent in an unnatural position.

"Eric!"

He didn't move as she was dragged inside the transport.

"Please help him! You have to help him!" she shouted.

The Alliance soldiers lifted her into the waiting transport where several other Praxton soldiers waited, some of them with minor injuries. One of the Alliance soldiers spoke to her in a calm but stern voice.

"Be quiet. We will take appropriate care of the injured. Now sit down and don't give us a reason to gag you. Understood?"

She looked up at him with tears welling into her eyes. "Yes sir, please sir."

The transport lifted off and gradually Lucinda took in the sight of the quiet soldiers that were in the GAAMV with her. She counted four missing. She looked at the Alliance soldiers wearing dark face shields that both protected their faces and hid any emotions. One was looking at her and she gradually took stock of her own self. Her top was pushed up at the bottom to just below her breasts, showing off her bare stomach. Her skirt hemline was sitting around her waist, and without any panties on, was exposing everything below her hips.

Lucinda immediately began to try to pull down her top but found it difficult with the restrictions on her hands. The Alliance guard noticed efforts and walked over to her.

The guard stood in front of her and a woman's voice spoke. "Normally prisoners are not allowed excessive movement, but this might qualify as special circumstances. Stand up."

Lucinda stood. The guard grabbed the hem of her skirt and pulled it down, covering Lucinda's exposed hips and sex. She then tugged down her top.

"Sit down now."

Lucinda sat. "Thank you. I hadn't realized my clothes had shifted so much."

"I think the men did." The voice was not unfriendly. "You may want to consider wearing underwear in the future."

"My boyfriend likes me to go without underwear."

"I'll bet he does. Doesn't mean you have to do it." The guard returned to her post.

Lucinda sighed, thinking, *Doesn't she understand that a female always listens to her boyfriend or guardian? Besides, I like going without underwear.*

Chapter Thirteen

Lloyd ran a finger over Nicole's nipples, as he surveyed her body.

"You know, Praxton customs dictate that I must discipline you," he said, as a statement of fact and not a question.

"I expect you to." She licked her lips. "I guess I want you to, as well."

He went to the dresser drawer and pulled out a whip. "Good. I know you'll be able to take this. You've already proven to me how tough you are."

She watched him play with the stands of the whip with his fingertips. "I will. I won't give in easily." Nicole wanted him to know she was prepared, that she wasn't scared of him.

"I wasn't born on Praxton and neither were you. I think, so far, we've both done a good job of following Praxton customs."

"We have." She watched him toy with the whip in his hands, and it looked like he was reluctant to use it on her. "I want you to use that whip on me, I want you to force me to submit to you." She took a deep breath. "I want the other females to look at my body and know you punished me, that I had no choice but to accept you as my guardian. I know you don't want to hurt me, but I can take it. I want it. Don't you want to use that whip on me at least a little bit?"

He hefted the whip in his hand and raised it. "You're right. I do want to whip you." He struck her on her breasts first and moved down, across her stomach. "Spread your legs."

Nicole spread her legs and then closed her eyes as he hit her inner thighs and then the outside of her legs. He whipped her lower legs and then moved up again, hitting close to her pussy, before striking her breasts again.

He stopped. "Turn around."

Nicole struggled to twist around on the chains holding her wrists above her.

The whip struck her back at the shoulders and moved down one side, reaching down to her foot. He grabbed her ankle, lifted her foot and struck her sole.

Nicole clenched her hands into fists and lowered her forehead to the wall.

He put down her foot and lifted her other ankle. "Had enough yet?"

Nicole shook her head and flinched as he struck the sole of that foot. He began to move the whip up her body. When he struck her ass, she whispered, "Okay, that's enough, please. I give in. I accept you as my guardian." Her knees began to bend. She called out louder, "I will submit to you. I will accept you as my guardian."

"You did well to make it through the discipline so far."

She turned her head. "So far?"

She felt his hands on her. One hand circled around to her front and his fingers pressed against her clit. She let out an involuntary moan.

"You're wet."

"I know. What did you expect?"

He used his other hand to smack her ass.

"Oh!"

Again, he struck her cheek while keeping his fingers inside her pussy.

"Oh!"

"You like that." He struck again. "Are you ready for the next step? To accept me as your guardian?"

"Yes, for crying out loud, I said that already. Yes!"

He lifted the chain off the hook and led her to the bed. "Kneel by the bed."

She quickly dropped to her knees and watched as he undressed. As soon as he removed his underwear, his cock jumped up.

He walked over to her and slid his cock over her lips. "I want you to take my whole cock if you can."

"I will. I want to." She worked her lips around the head and slowly drew it into her mouth. Her tongue danced around his cock as he slid it deeper into her mouth and finally into her throat. Nicole gasped as he pumped his cock in and out. She used her tongue as much as she could, wanting him to come as soon as possible.

After he came, she continued to suck on him, wanting to show him she was ready for more.

He grabbed her by her hair, pulled her to the bed and ordered her to lie on her back with her hands above her head.

She immediately obeyed. "Yes Master Lloyd."

Gallagher went to the dresser and took out several items from the drawer. He returned to her, locking a cuff on her ankle, and then attached a chain from it to the foot of the bed. He placed a matching cuff on her other ankle, but didn't restrain it with a chain, merely locking it as well with a small padlock. He then took a chain, attached it to one of her wrists cuffs and locked the other end to the headboard.

"I always found nipple clamps attractive, especially these types that have a chain between them."

"I've worn those types before but my nipples are a bit sensitive."

"Then this may hurt a bit." He frowned. "You're not objecting are you?"

"Oh, no, Master Lloyd. If that is what you wish I will bear it."

He clamped the silver devices on her nipples slowly, waited until she clenched her jaw and then gave it another small tightening. "There, you look helpless and very sexy."

"Thank you." She squirmed a bit in her restraints.

"I have a ball gag here as well." He dangled it in front of her. "What do you think of wearing one?"

Nicole licked her lips. "I think it would make me even more helpless. You should make me wear it." She watched him place the ball gag at her mouth. "Master Lloyd, I believe I need another spanking as well. I liked it when you had your fingers in my pussy last time."

"Of course my sweet..." He pushed the ball into her mouth and tightened the buckle behind her head. He then pushed her hips and she rolled onto her stomach.

Nicole felt his fingers work under her and inserted into her clit. Seconds later, his palm came down on her cheeks, peppering her ass with smacks. She tried to moan through her gag, gurgling out sounds as she suddenly climaxed. She couldn't stop her hips from rising and falling as he spanked her. She whimpered as she became exhausted.

Gallagher rolled her over, looking at her heaving breasts. "Now it's my turn again." He plunged his cock into her wet pussy, hammering it deep inside her.

Nicole tugged at the chain holding her hands above her head, relishing the feeling of being forced. There was nothing she could do, even to speak, to stop him from fulfilling his own pleasure. She climaxed again before he was finished.

Gallagher relaxed a few seconds on top of her and then rolled off her. A minute later, he took off her ball gag. "How do you feel now?"

"Wonderful."

He looked at her naked body stretched out by his side. "Your skin has pink stripes all over it. It looks like you got a good whipping."

"Good. The other females will be jealous of how hard you had to work to claim me. I bet my bum is red after that spanking. How many times did you spank me today? Four?"

"I think so. I do believe you like being spanked."

She laughed. "I do, I do. I don't know why, but I really like it when... well I have this fantasy that you have my hands cuffed behind my back and I'm lying helpless over your lap, naked of course. You spank me hard in front of a room full of people. I don't know why I have to have people witness my spanking, but hey, it's my fantasy."

"I could go along with that fantasy." He grinned. "Of course, I may add nipple clamps and a crotch rope as well."

"A crotch rope? That would make it...interesting. I think you're trying to change my fantasy to one of yours."

"No, just supplementing it."

"Okay, I'll take the nipple clamps, but not the crotch rope with the spanking."

"I think the crotch rope adds something."

"Yeah, it does. Okay, I'll amend my fantasy to include the crotch rope too. But it better be a good spanking."

He leaned over her and ran his hand over her breasts. "Maybe I should undo your wrists from the headboard."

She looked up. "You don't have to. I'm enjoying this moment."

He kissed her. "So am I."

Chapter Fourteen

The Alliance Military station maintained a synchronous orbit around Praxton. Captain Lois Chapman was in charge of decks four through eight, where supplies and prisoners were kept. It had proven to be a more interesting assignment than she expected.

She made her way down to deck seven, where the female prisoners were kept, and stopped at the duty desk where the sergeant saluted her.

"I understand there are problems with the prisoners."

"Yes, ma'am," Maxine Smyth reported. "The female prisoners are acting very strange, and while they are not trying to break out, they are causing some concern."

"Are they refusing to obey orders or eat?"

"No, actually they are very compliant. If they are told to do anything, they act immediately. It seems they are well conditioned to authorities."

"Then the problem is...?"

The cell they are in holds six prisoners. The females use only three beds, and they are narrow beds. They also sleep nude, and well, they haven't had sexual intercourse, yet there is a lot of, umm, touching, kissing. They also give each other frequent pats on the ass. I don't know if this is acceptable or not. In any event, how do you wish we handle it?"

Chapman sighed. "They aren't having any unusual problems with the male prisoners. "I'll see what's going on."

"There's also a situation that they are usually naked, and it's causing some problems with our guards."

"I'll look into that too."

"Thank you, ma'am. Oh, one other thing is they all want to leave their collars on, so we let them."

"Oh, great. Trained females."

She looked at the six females on the other side of the heavy wired screen and entered the cell. A male guard stood outside, looking at the female prisoners. Two were wearing the orange prisoner coveralls, while another two wore only the next-to-nothing Praxton panties they were wearing when brought to the station. The other two were nude and were sitting on a bed. One was comforting the other in her arms.

"Which one of you is the ranking officer?"

The nude female comforting the other spoke. "I am, Warrant Officer, Jillian Scott."

Where should she start? "May I ask why you are naked and not wearing the coveralls?"

"We are used to being nude and find the coveralls uncomfortable. On Praxton females are often nude in confined rooms, especially cages or cells."

"Alright, but you're on Alliance property now. How would you feel about having your uniforms returned to you?"

"That would be okay. But we don't mind being naked."

"Yes, but it is causing a problem with my male crew here. And some of the female crew as well."

"Very well, if that's what you require us to do."

She shook her head. "I'm not forcing you to do so. Here on Alliance worlds, we believe in individual freedom."

"Is that why Praxton was attacked and we were taken prisoner?"

"No, we want to free you and other females."

"We were free. Now we're not."

"You're wearing a collar. Correct me if I'm wrong, doesn't that make you a slave to men?"

She shook her head. "No, I can remove the collar at any time. I want to wear it. It means I'm wanted by a guardian." She pointed at a bracelet Chapman was wearing. "Did a male give you that jewellery?"

"Yes, my husband."

"Guardians give us these collars. They mean the same thing to us as your bracelet, a ring or a necklace. These collars mean everything to us right now."

"Okay, if that's what you want." She fingered her bracelet,

understanding the comparison.

"It has also been observed you are all sleeping in pairs, in the nude."

"None of us ever wear anything when sleeping. It's how females sleep. On Praxton there's a shortage of men, so females sleep together for companionship. We enjoy the comfort of another body. If you want, I can promise there won't be any sex, if that makes you feel better."

"Thank you. I'd appreciate that, at least."

The female she was comforting suddenly spoke up. "How is Master Eric? Is he alright? Can I see him please?"

"Master Eric?"

"Lucinda means Corporal Eric Winston. He was injured and was on our ship."

"None of your crew members were killed. Some are receiving medical attention. I will check the reports and confirm he is doing okay."

"He was going to be my guardian, and I'm so worried about him."

"I'll pass that on." She smiled. "He's lucky to have someone like you so worried about him."

Lucinda wiped away a tear. "Why did you have to invade us? We want Praxton to remain the way it is, was. No one asked for you to come and destroy our world."

Jillian gave her a kiss on her forehead and turned back to Chapman. "Praxton is fine the way it is. Females are content and happy, the ones with guardians that is. If they don't like Praxton, they can immigrate to Alliance worlds. But Praxton has one of the highest standards of living and one of the lowest crime rates. Females wearing a collar are never harassed by men. We can go and do what we want. Can Alliance females say the same everywhere?"

Chapman nodded. "Your point is taken. But the decision to help Praxton was not mine to make. I will have those clothes sent to you."

"Thank you. Could I ask you for some makeup for us well? We're used to getting ourselves prepared each morning to look right."

Chapman resisted rolling her eyes. "I will see what I can do."

Chapman walked slowly to back to her office. Her first thought, that the females were merely brainwashed, was discarded, and she began to question the whole mission to invade Praxton. She knew that Praxton society was going to be changed and made poorer because of it. Other worlds the Alliance had taken over because of the lack of compliance to the Charter of Conduct had suffered as a result. She sat at her desk and typed out a requisition for the female uniforms to be returned. Alliance military thought that taking away their uniforms and giving them coveralls to wear would make the transition of leaving the Praxton culture easier. Chapman thought it was a ridiculous idea at the time and was glad to put an end to it.

A flashing light began to blink, indicating an incoming message.

"Emergency meeting at fourteen hundred hours, room 2B21..."

She acknowledged the message, and then sent another message to the infirmary, inquiring the status of Corporal Eric Winston.

* * * *

Nicole woke up and needed a few seconds to orientate herself. Her hands were cuffed behind her back and a chain held her ankle to the foot of the bed. She shifted to a new position, looked around the empty room and tried to guess what time it was. She carefully moved to a sitting position, finding her ass was still sore from the spanking last night.

In the middle of the night, Lloyd had decided to change her restraints and joined her wrist cuffs behind her back. He used a chain from her collar to the cuffs to pull them up her back. He spanked her once more before ordering her to take his cock in her mouth again. She quickly obeyed.

When he was hard enough again he entered her pussy once more, squeezing her breasts as he pounded inside her.

The memories of the late night sex came to her, and she sighed softly, even though her body ached from the whipping. She wished she could remove the nipple clamps. He had loosened the clamps later, but her breasts and nipples were sore and the weight was pulling down on them.

She waited for several minutes and then called out, "Hello, anyone there?"

Another ten minutes passed before Angela appeared. "Good morning."

"Good morning. Where is Master Lloyd?"

"He is meeting with some Praxton officials and should be back at lunchtime. In the meantime, he instructed me to get you ready for the day." She giggled. "He was quite specific."

Nicole relaxed in the large tub, letting the water and oil sooth her skin. In a few minutes, she knew she would have to get out and wear what was set out for her. It seemed she was going to have to get used to wearing cuffs and chains that restricted her movements. He had also left her only a single garment to wear: a black lace dress with an open weave.

Nicole sighed as the warm water surged around her and gently felt her nipples, finding they weren't as sore as she expected from the nipple clamps.

Angela entered the room and informed her it was time to get ready. Nicole nodded and stepped out of the tub, dried herself off and then sat at a table to apply cream on her face, then makeup. She attached the cuffs and matching metal collar, locked them and picked up a pair of silver coloured nipple jewellery. They were triangular shaped and joined by a thin chain. She carefully eased them on, and they forced her sensitive nipples to project forward.

The dress she simply slipped over her head. It was short and became even shorter when the belt was attached, short enough to cause a bit of a problem when she sat down. The wide belt had a series of metal rings around it so that chains could be attached to her cuffs. Nicole looked at the chains, wishing she didn't have to use them but attached them. They were short enough to restrict her arm movements, and the ankle cuffs also had a chain between them.

She stood in front of a viewscreen and noticed her body was readily visible under the dress with her nipples protruding. She noticed the locks and chains on her cuffs and collar gave her a vulnerable look, and she decided that she actually liked what she saw. *It does look sexy. Even it is a bit uncomfortable. Anyway, if this is what he wants, then I'll do it.*

Nicole carefully walked downstairs, and went to the dining room where she heard several people talking. They greeted her, and soon she was accepting congratulations.

One of the females called out, "Did you put up decent fight? Was he strong enough?"

"Yes and yes he was."

"Prove it." Another female got up from her chair and walked over. "Let's see proof."

A second female got up as well and the two of them began to pull up her dress. Nicole resisted for a moment, giggling as her belt was undone and her dress was lifted up. They pulled her dress up to her shoulders.

"Look at those marks. Turn around."

Nicole turned around and the other females clapped and cheered at the red marks on her body. Several made a comment on how red her bottom was.

"Okay, you've seen the proof. Can I get dressed again?"

"Maybe, if you give us some more details about last night."

"Let's just say I find even this cushioned chair uncomfortable to sit on, and he doesn't like my hands free." Nicole put her dress and belt back on.

That admission led to even more chatter and jokes, but Nicole stopped at giving any more information.

Sophie, one of the other females she'd traveled with, had an amused grin as she asked Nicole another question. "Now, I had the impression you liked being a freelancer, and didn't want to ever wear a collar, let alone accept a guardian. What exactly happened on that walk through the desert?"

Nicole blushed and looked down at her plate as everyone stared at her. She swallowed and looked up. She wondered how she could tell them when it happened, when he first forced her to her knees when she was captured, and then collared her. She became seduced by his strength to dominate her and later when he took compassion on her during the walk to the transport. Now, for the first time since she arrived on Praxton, she found wearing restrains erotic. Nicole knew this was a man she could respect, and one that could take care of her.

"Nothing special other than it gave me time to think and to understand what wearing a guardian's collar really means."

Sophie giggled, "I think there's more to that story than you're telling. But congratulations."

Chapter Fifteen

The meeting wasn't long. The six captains in attendance were told that a minor security breach had occurred at the communication satellite with encrypted information bypassing the usual buffers. The short burst was not likely to give any military advantage to Praxton, as they didn't have any allies that were willing to aid them in the conflict. However, a message was sent out and received between Praxton and one of the Alliance worlds. The site of the signal source was not known.

The Alliance military had control of most of Praxton, but the Praxton military was still fighting in small areas. So far, both militaries had stayed out of the cities where civilian populations would be at risk.

Lois Chapman listened to the reports, reflecting how the expectations of the general population, especially the females, would happily greet the arrival of the Alliance military and the introduction of the Charter of Conduct document. The unusual fighting techniques of the Praxton military, and the resistance of the population to a change in their way of life, were making the conquest much slower than they expected.

Chapman left the meeting deciding she wanted to learn more about Praxton's way of life, and why they resisted the arrival of the Alliance military. She went back to her office and used her computer to search the Praxton history, and brought up acceptable female behaviour on present day. She learned that on present day Praxton, a female must obey her guardian and was expected to not only wear his collar, but to accept lockable cuffs and chains. However, what the Alliance worlds and the Charter of Conduct did not make known was that females could leave their guardians if they chose.

The wearing of the collar was very symbolic of his control and his obligation to make her safe and cared for. The cuffs and chains were also representative of his control, but had also become fashion accessories.

Chapman began to wonder how a society entrenched with the female under male control would be willing to accept the Charter of Conduct and its laws that enforced Earth's society behaviour. The females on Praxton were happy and content with the way they lived, and no amount of military conquest was going to change that.

She left her office for the evening feeling troubled.

* * * *

Lloyd Gallagher returned to the house and Nicole ran to the front door to greet him. After a series of kisses, he walked with her to the living room where he sat down with Master Alex, Angela, and most of the other people in the household.

"Alex here was good enough to introduce me to Romie Crocetti, one of your nearby neighbours. It seems he, and a female under his care, have sent a message to Alliance worlds. The message contains, among other things, a video that has brought pressure on the Alliance military to cease hostilities. It seems the general Alliance population is protesting the invasion of Praxton. I guess the video is being widely seen, partly due to some of the female actors in it. If I understand correctly, some of you were in that video."

Several of the females nodded or murmured an affirmative.

"I took a copy of the transmission and you can look at it later. The message was broadcast and sent around the Alliance worlds and apparently is a hot topic in newscasts. Suffice to say, there is now mounting pressure by the media for the Charter of Conduct Office and the Alliance military to let Praxton be free to choose their own form of society.

"What I must do is to relay this message on to the remaining Praxton military, and let them know, if they can continue to fight and resist the complete take over of Praxton, we may be able to force the Alliance worlds to negotiate."

Nicole looked glum. "You're going away?"

"I have to." He squeezed her hand and looked into her eyes.

Angela waited to speak until he turned his attention back to the group. "Do you wish for me to look after Nicole?"

"Yes please. I have received permission from Alex that Nicole and the rest of the females may stay here as long as they need to, provided they accept Angela as the senior female."

The remaining five females Gallagher was escorting nodded their assent. If Alex had insisted they accept him as their guardian, it would mean they could be bedded by him at any time as well as being forced to wear his collar. That would make staying in his household a difficult one. Instead, Angela was going to be the one they had to obey, which meant Alex didn't have direct control over them nor was he responsible for their actions.

After the meeting, Gallagher and Nicole had a separate meeting with Angela to discuss how Nicole was to be treated.

"I understand Nicole was a freelancer until she recently accepted you as a guardian?"

"Yes she was. She is a little headstrong."

Angela nodded. "I'm sure we can take care of that, if the need arises. She will have to get used to being under control."

Nicole spoke in a quiet voice. "When I first arrived here on Praxton, I had a guardian, but he was cruel and liked to use devices and the whip a little too much. That is why I became a freelancer."

Angela shook her head. "You should have given another guardian a chance first before taking a chance on being a freelancer. There have been serious situations for some of those females."

"I understand that now. But now, I accept Master Lloyd as my guardian."

Angela looked at Gallagher. "How do you wish for Nicole to be handled?"

"I want her to get used to wearing cuffs and chains. Every day she should wear ankle and wrist cuffs with chains for several hours. I would also need her to get used to a leash again."

Nicole resisted letting out a sigh of disapproval.

"And discipline Master Lloyd?"

"What you feel is required. I do believe it would be appropriate to have her spend some time in a cage and to be spanked."

Angela nodded. "I certainly agree with you there. Is she allowed to wear clothes?"

"Yes, I believe she is already comfortable with her looks and being nude around others."

"Excellent. One final question, do you have a preference which female she sleeps with?"

"No, though it might be good for her to enjoy the company of different females."

Nicole listened to the conversation between Gallagher and Angela. Her opinion and input wasn't needed, though she was glad she wasn't going to be retrained by Angela. That would have involved strong discipline and humiliation in front of the others in the household. It appeared that if she behaved, Angela was allowed to give her some freedom. Nicole wasn't happy to hear she would be spending time in a cage again. Her memories of how she was used when she was in a cage under her first guardian weren't pleasant, but she felt Angela wasn't going to be abusive.

Nicole gave Gallagher a long kiss goodbye and watched him and Sergeant Wilson leave. She stood at the front door after it closed and stared at it. Angela touched her on the shoulder and clipped a leash on her collar.

"Come with me. Master Lloyd will be back in a few days, but until then, you can spend the time learning how to act properly for him."

"What if he gets hurt or killed?"

"Don't think about that. You can't change what may happen by worrying about it."

Nicole nodded and followed her. "Where are we going?"

"To the garden out back. I think what you need more than anything right now is to relax and have a glass of wine."

"That does sound good."

Nicole sat on the small bench on the patio facing the flower garden. Her leash had been removed and she waited a few minutes for Angela to return with two glasses of wine.

"Here you go."

"Thank you." Nicole took the offered glass.

Angela sat next to her. "I'm curious. How much influence did the war with Alliance forces have on your decision to have a guardian again?"

Nicole looked at Angela and listened carefully to her tone of voice. She didn't detect any hostility in her question or resentment from her being a freelancer before. "Well maybe there was the sub-conscious part in it, but I truly did fall for Master Lloyd. It was during the training exercise that I saw his strength, compassion and character when he forced me to surrender. Before the hostilities started, I already had agreed to wear his collar. I guess somewhere in the desert when he had all six of us females handcuffed and chained together, that I realized being in cuffs and chains under the right man wasn't so bad. From there I knew I wanted to get a commitment from him to be my guardian. Does that answer your question?"

"Yes. It does mean you have accepted the role of a female on Praxton."

"It does. You know, he was hesitant to use the whip on me last night. I told him I wanted to be whipped."

"He was scared he would hurt you?"

"At first, but then he got right into it. I wanted to have marks on my body, because I knew the other females would want to see them to see how strong he was or how weak I was. I know they thought of me as a freelancer trying to pose as a Praxton female just for protection. That's not true, I am a Praxton female now, but I needed to prove that I was as tough as they were."

"I think you did that. They saw the remains of the whip marks and how red your bottom was."

Nicole blushed. "He really spanked me a lot yesterday. I expect more of that in the future too."

"Tonight, I thought you could sleep with me." She placed a hand on Nicole's thigh. "I promise to make sure we don't abuse your skin anymore."

"Thanks. I have to tell you since I became a freelancer, I haven't had to sleep with many females, so it will take a bit for me to get used to."

"I'll be careful." She leaned over and gave Nicole a kiss on her lips. "More wine?"

Chapter Sixteen

Captain Lois Chapman pushed herself away from her desk. *I think I'm going to have to do a little of my own investigating of this Praxton culture.*

The reports coming from the military forces were not what were expected when they launched the attacks on Praxton. At first, the Praxton military had given the Alliance forces trouble with a defence designed strictly for fighting on or near the desert surface. The GAAMV aircraft were still hiding and launching QUACK weapons in the large desert areas of Praxton, depriving the Alliance forces of claiming complete control and victory. Ironically, the second problem for the Alliance forces was one of the clauses in the Charter of Conduct, the document that the Alliance Forces used to justify an attack on Praxton.

The Charter of Conduct forbade hard interrogation of captured enemy soldiers, stipulating the length of time of solitary confinement, physical and psychological treatment as well as food and water. It also forbade attacking and damaging civilian property or risking civilians' health, unless forced to do so by engagement with enemy soldiers. The Praxton military had apparently been aware of this, and moved military personnel out of the cities. Also, they had moved the key government leaders to hidden desert locations.

It meant the battle for Praxton had to be fought against the Praxton forces in the desert, a slow and expensive exercise. The cities, towns and farmland were left alone, except for minor investigations. When the Alliance forces tried to contact the civilians, especially the females, to let them know they were being saved from an unpopular government and being set free, they were met with anger and defiance. It seemed the

169

Praxton people did not want to change from their present laws and social customs. After several futile efforts, the Alliance Forces withdrew from any contact with civilians and their cities.

Chapman went down to the holding cells of the female prisoners. She was pleased to see the prisoners were wearing the clothes provided for them, at least during the daytime. It seemed they were going to stick stubbornly to their practice of sleeping nude and in the company of another female.

"Private Lucinda Taylor?"

The dark haired woman looked up from where she sat on the edge of a bed. "Yes, Captain Chapman?"

Chapman reflected on how the female prisoners were respectful to figures of authority and obeyed almost any order given by the guards. The same couldn't be said of the male prisoners who were acting like most prisoners of war. There were only a few male prisoners in the infirmary, but they were causing some difficulties with the nursing staff.

"I have some free time this afternoon, and was wondering if you would like to accompany me to the infirmary and see Corporal Eric Winston?"

She jumped up. "Yes, yes, yes!" She turned to the senior female, Warrant Officer Jillian Scott. "May I please go, Jillian?"

Jillian smiled. "Of course."

Later that afternoon when Chapman returned to take Lucinda with her she could see she had carefully applied her makeup and brushed her hair. She had also expected Lucinda to want to half run down the hallway once she stepped out of the cell. But she slowly walked with a gentle sway of hips that Praxton females were well known for. Chapman looked at the female guard that was accompanying them and noticed she was taking a couple of glances at their prisoner. Coupled with the walk, the short skirt, the tight top without a bra underneath and high heel boots, Lucinda made an interesting sight as she walked.

They rode the elevator to the infirmary ward and Chapman watched the Praxton female practically jump up and down waiting for the doors to open. Once the doors opened, she again resumed her slow walk to the nursing station.

Chapman addressed the nurse at the station. "This is the POW that is to visit a Praxton soldier, a Corporal Eric Winston.

The nurse took her eyes off Lucinda and looked down on her monitor. "He is in room 5719."

"Thank you."

"Doctor Fogelman will be joining you there. I will page her."

Lucinda hugged Eric tight as he sat up on his hospital bed and then kissed him several times on his lips and face. Chapman and Captain Olencia Fogelman, the ship's medical doctor, stood just inside the patient's room, watching. The two were friends on board the spaceship, and both were speculating how the Praxton invasion was going to turn out.

"So they are obviously happy to see each other."

Olencia laughed. "That, apparently, is the first time he's been happy since being here."

"I hear he's been a bit rude to the nurses."

"Well, to be fair, he was in a lot of pain at first. His leg was broken in three places and his back was a mess too. But he refused to do anything they asked him unless it was phrased as a request. The nurses complained about his arrogant attitude."

"They didn't care for him much?" Lois turned her attention to Olencia.

"He didn't endear himself to them when he asked where their collars were."

"Oh, that wouldn't go over well. He's lucky he's getting any care at all."

"The funny thing is there's no shortage of nurses quite willing to bring him his medication. I guess they find him a challenge and enjoy his offhand comments."

"Interesting. Let's take his lady friend to the coffee room and ask her a few questions." She walked up to Lucinda and touched her on her arm.

"Time to go."

Eric spoke. "It's all right, Lucinda, you can go with her. Remember I'm going to collar you when this is all over."

"Yes Master Eric, I look forward to wearing your collar."

Chapman exchanged a look with Fogelman.

171

The two captains and Lucinda sat in the coffee room located by the nursing station.

Lois gave Lucinda a cup of tea and sat at the table. "So tell me, did I hear that he is going to collar you? What exactly does that mean?"

Lucinda grinned, happy to provide details. "It means I'm going to wear a collar he provides. Usually, the male will also provide matching cuffs. He will lock the corner, which means he'll care for me, protect me and discipline me. When I wear his collar, it's also a sign to other males that I'm spoken for."

"But what does he wear as a symbol?"

Lucinda looked puzzled. "Nothing. He still can go after other females and collar them."

"Men are allowed to do that? You don't care?" Olencia spoke up.

"Of course I'd rather be his only female, but men always want to have more than one female. Don't Alliance men want to have more than one female?"

"Yes. But as a woman, I won't allow my man to do so, and he knows it."

Lucinda shrugged. "Then maybe either your man is frustrated, or not telling you everything he does. Men are men and they are always looking at another woman."

As Olencia pursed her lips, Lois tried another question.

"So does this mean Eric is now your guardian?"

Lucinda shook her head. "No. Not yet. After I wear his collar for a period of time and I please him, he will offer to become my guardian. If I accept, I then move into his household. That means he is then also responsible for me financially."

"So, that is like a marriage we have on Alliance worlds?" Lois asked.

"No, after being my guardian, he may propose we perform the Affinity Ceremony, which is closer to your marriage, but more serious. As my guardian, I can remove his collar at any time and walk away from him after I write a statement informing him of my decision to do so, and have it witnessed. A guardian is responsible financially for my well-being, so I have to announce that he is free of any obligations towards me. He can also ask me to return his collar and find a different guardian.

After the Affinity Ceremony, it requires the signature of a judge to break the agreement. It is very rare for that to happen, Affinity is for life and isn't done lightly."

Olencia swirled her tea in her cup as she asked another question. "You said something about discipline earlier."

"Yes, that can mean a variety of things. Not allowing me to shop, spanking, whipping, caging or whatever he thinks appropriate. He can't physically cause permanent damage, and usually, most discipline is mild. Spanking is the most common, but isn't just for discipline, it's also a sign of affection."

"A sign of affection?" Olencia asked, slightly shocked.

"Yes. For example, he'll have me lie over his lap and give me a light spanking. It shows he's still in control and cares for me. It's also usually a prelude to sex." She looked at Olencia. "Have you ever been spanked or given a few light pats on your ass by your man?"

Olencia blushed. "The odd time he may give me a few swats on my ass, but I'm standing and fully dressed."

"Don't you find the thought of lying naked over his lap enticing? Like if it happened and he spanked you lightly, wouldn't you enjoy that?"

Olencia opened her mouth to say something, but changed her mind.

"You do, don't you? Just that, on Praxton, we admit we like our men being dominant."

Olencia was glad for a chance to change the subject. "We on Alliance world prefer our men to more caring and gentle."

"Really? So the most popular men on Alliance world aren't ones with power, strength and in control of those around them? I saw an Alliance news report a few weeks ago of screaming females greeting this actor who was known for treating his females poorly. Seems to me Alliance women prefer men who are strong and in control too. On Praxton we're just open about it. Thing is, you can't have a strong man and then try controlling him in a relationship. That just leads to frustration on both sides."

Lois broke into the conversation. "Why don't you say goodbye to Eric? You have two minutes, no more."

"Thank you, Captain." She quickly stood and walked slowly to his room.

Lois and Olencia followed her.

Olencia looked at the walk of Lucinda and whispered to Lois, "Quite the walk in the short skirt and high heels. They sure are aware how to dress and act for men."

"That's true. But after listening to talk about Praxton, do you think we have a chance of converting Praxton to an Alliance world?"

"No, and the damnedest thing is she really seems to understand men and women. It makes me wonder if she might be half right."

Lois laughed. "Like you getting a spanking?"

Olencia laughed back. "I'm not saying that, but like I said, she might be right on a few things."

They watched Eric gently stroke her back as she hugged him, and then Lois led her back to her cell.

Captain Olencia Fogelman walked over to Winston's bed. "So you're feeling better?"

"Yes, especially after seeing Lucinda."

"She was very worried about you. You're a lucky man."

"I suppose so." He gave her a shrug. "But you're not really interested in making small talk are you?"

"I'm just curious about you. The nurses here say you are rude, but obviously Lucinda thinks highly of you."

"Sorry, don't mean to be rude. I never had to obey commands from a female before. It was difficult to adjust to."

"That's understandable. Do you feel they don't respect you?"

"I doubt that they do. They are Alliance nurses. I'm a Praxton soldier. I sensed they weren't amused that I represent Praxton society."

"Maybe you have to find a better way to obtain a woman's respect besides whipping her."

He grinned. "You were waiting how long to say that? Come on, Doctor, how can you criticize something you only have read about through the propaganda of the Charter of Conduct Office? You have never seen a whipping, let alone received one. How do you know exactly what it is about?"

"I don't have to be hit by a laser blast to know it's painful."

"True. But laser blast is intended to inflict damage on a person. A whipping I'm talking about is a prelude to sex and prepares the female for the pleasure she is to receive."

"I doubt that very much."

"Really? How about a bet? I get to whip you or any female on this floor, and if she isn't wet after fifteen minutes I'll resign from the Praxton military. If she is wet, you resign from the Alliance military."

She glared at him. "That's...that's ridiculous."

"Why? Because you know I'm right?"

"Just because a woman is wet, as you so indelicately put it, doesn't mean she actually enjoying it or should be whipped."

"Bullshit. She's enjoying it and you know it. I know females and can tell when they are feeling pleasure."

"This is getting us nowhere." She turned to leave.

"Wait. I think what you have is a misconception of what the whip is."

She turned back to him. "Enlighten me."

"It has a multi-strand thong. Each strand is made of a lightweight, flat material. When it strikes the female's skin, it is designed to make it tingle. It doesn't really hurt any more than a light spanking. You've had one of those before haven't you?"

Fogelman blushed. "Never mind, I'll consider your explanation." She walked to the door and turned around. "But if you want women to respect you, you have to respect them."

He laughed. "I would love to collar you."

She opened her mouth in surprise and quickly walked out of the room.

* * * *

Lieutenant Lloyd Gallagher sat with Sergeant Doug Wilson on the two-seat all-terrain transport. The six wheeled open cab vehicle was borrowed from one of the residents and was used to explore the desert. The vehicle was originally built to do farm work and had a large bed in the back designed to hold bulky items. The electric motor whined as Wilson pushed the power near its maximum. Both men wore borrowed civilian clothes in case the Alliance forces checked on what they were doing out in the desert.

They sped across the desert, going around the rocky outcroppings and sand dunes. It would have been quicker to use the sand and gravel road that ran to the base camp from the residential area, but that might have drawn suspicion to them faster than driving around in the desert as a pair of bored Praxton citizens.

As Wilson drove, Gallagher studied the LCD screen that indicated where the highest elevation point in the desert was located. That point was one of the rocky islands in the desert. The vast desert areas of Praxton, like many deserts, had sand dunes drifting across its surface, but the geology also produced outcrops of rocky surface. The red rock lifted above the desert surface, occasionally forming a maze of paths through the rock. On some islands, porous red columns stood as well, a reminder of a time the desert was under a vast sea.

The Alliance Forces had effectively reduced most radio communication to static, but Gallagher had a transmitter that could send out a powerful burst of their signal. It would be more effective if they could place the antenna at a high point and that was their intention.

They had driven for half an hour when the large, dark, rectangular shape of an Alliance Forces ship descended above them. They felt the low vibration hum through their bodies as they looked up at the ship that bristled with weapons. The ship hovered above them before moving a short distance away and landing on six short legs with sand with dust blowing out from below.

Four armed soldiers left the ship and walked to Wilson and Gallagher. Two soldiers spread out from the others two with guns aimed. Wilson and Gallagher sat still in the vehicle with their hands visible.

The soldier in charged barked out questions, "What are you doing out here? Are you two spying?"

Gallagher shook his head. "No sir. We're civilians, not connected to the military."

"Then what in blazes are you doing out in the desert? Don't you two know there are hostilities and this area is a hell of a dangerous place to be in?"

"Yes sir. But we're geologists and have to complete our study or else we'll break our contract."

"Geologists? If you really are, then you tell me how those columns are formed."

"Well you have to understand that this was a shallow sea at one time. Underneath the floor of the sea, heat forced lava to rise and made islands form. The lava was largely composed of iron and that is why we have the reddish rock. Also, from under the seafloor, sea geysers of hot steam carried particles of iron ore upward and then rapidly cooled from the seawater. The result is the columns." Gallagher had listened to his parents often enough to know what formed the columns and the islands.

"Alright then. But be aware you are in danger of incidental fire in this area. I would advise you to keep your visit as short as possible."

Gallagher waited until the soldiers returned to the ship and turned to Wilson. "I wasn't too surprised we were stopped, and it looks like they don't suspect us as anything but civilians. Let's make tracks. We have about eight kilometres to go."

They reached the island a half hour later, its rocky surface rising above the desert sand with the columns towering above the landscape. Wilson and Gallagher carried the equipment, twisting around the misshapen rocks.

Gallagher stopped at one of the columns and looked up at its top. "I guess one is as good as another. You want to climb it or do I?"

"I've done a lot of tree climbing as a kid. This doesn't look much different."

Wilson slung the transmitter over his back and proceeded to climb the meter diameter column. The porous rock made it easy to find hand and foot grips, and he soon reached the top. Using a rope, he secured the transmitter to the top and then carefully lowered himself down.

Gallagher in the meantime had set up the broadcast equipment, setting a delay timer for the broadcast.

Wilson watched him latch the cover of the equipment. "So how much delay did you set it for?"

"One hour. It won't take long for the Alliance to find the source of the transmission and not much longer after that to figure out who set it up. They'll be somewhat pissed, but we should be out of the desert by then."

They hustled back to their vehicle and drove quickly back to where the desert ended. An hour later a repeating message began to broadcast in short, high-powered bursts.

Chapter Seventeen

Diane rested on the bed in her cage. Her skin tingled everywhere. She wished she could touch herself, but with her wrists cuffed behind her back, she could only try to make herself comfortable on the narrow cot. She felt aroused and when she gazed at the pink whip marks on her breasts, her nipples became erect.

She heard a noise and saw LeBlanc enter the room.

He opened the cage door. "How are you feeling?"

"Good, Master Troy." She rolled over to her side and swung her feet to the floor.

LeBlanc touched one nipple lightly and then squeezed her breast. "You feel very warm."

Diane moaned. "Yes, Master Troy."

He took her leash. "Come. It's time to go to my suite."

She followed him naked to the elevator where he again used his ID to order the elevator to take them directly to the top floor, where his suite was located.

Diane kept quiet during the time it took to reach his suite. When they arrived, he sat her in the living room, unlocked her wrist cuffs, but attached the leash to the back of her armchair. He poured her a glass of wine and sat in a chair across from her.

"Did you enjoy your time in the cage? Did it make you feel captive and wanted?"

"I enjoyed it, Master Troy and yes I did like the feeling of being your captive."

"Good. On Praxton I have heard many females express the desire to be pursued, be captured and taken by a male." He swirled the wine in glass, studying it and then looking back at her. "I have pursued you,

179

chased you down. I used words as my weapon of course. I believed you secretly wanted to be captured, even when you tried to refuse to wear a collar the first time."

"Really? I thought I rejected the collar rather strongly the first time."

"Too strongly, as if you were scared that by wearing one, your true feelings would come out."

"I suppose you were right there, Master Troy."

"I also noted your interest in the customs of Praxton. For example, when I took you on a tour in the basement I saw that you were in deep thought when I told you how females would be put on display on Reconciliation Day. I believed at that point I could convert you to the Praxton way of life."

"You have converted me."

He grinned. "But what if the Alliance Forces wins the day? Would you stay here on Praxton with me if the collars, cuffs and submission are banned?"

"No matter what the law is, Master Troy, I will submit to your wishes."

"That is good to hear. There have been reports." He paused for a moment, then said, "There is no need for me to be secretive to you. There has been a broadcast that originated here on Praxton that stated that a video supporting Praxton has been circulating around Alliance worlds. Apparently this has put enormous pressure on the Alliance government to stop the hostilities."

"So there is a chance of Praxton remaining free?"

"A small one. I suspect there will some negotiations, and Praxton will have to give up something, but can remain a free world."

"That is good news."

"Indeed it is." He stood up and took her leash from the back of her chair. "We will now go to the bedroom."

* * * *

Lois Chapman hurried down the hall for the latest unscheduled meeting. *Why do we have to meet in the same room for these announcements? Haven't they heard of computer links?*

She sat down and opened her notepad as she waited for the meeting to begin.

General Norman Cobalt looked at the six captains sitting around the table. He stood and then paced in front of the large viewscreen. He took a deep breath. "Ladies and gentlemen, I don't how to say this, so I'm going to just say it.

"We, as you all are well aware, have had a difficult time pinning down the Praxton forces. They are like desert rats scurrying to hide under rocks. No offence meant to the desert rats. Unfortunately, that leaked transmission last week has caused us problems. One, it turned the general Alliance population into thinking the planet Praxton should be left alone. And two, a radio communication here went to the Praxton troops informing them that there was political pressure on us to end this conflict. That seemed to inspire the Praxton troops to continue their fight even more."

He took a drink of water. "Unlike you sitting around here, I had to go and explain to General Burgess why this mission has been an abominable failure. It turns out that negotiations are going to commence twenty hours from now. At that time hostilities will cease. Any questions?"

Lois Chapman waited until the Captains with active troops had their questions answered and then ventured with one of her own. "If we are now negotiating peace terms, can I assume the release of prisoners of war will not be far behind?"

"That is correct. I suspect that will occur at the end of the first day of negotiations as a sign of good will. So be prepared for some sort of prisoner release in thirty hours."

* * * *

"I was getting annoyed with him already, and then he told me he wanted to collar me! I walked out of the room without saying another word to him." Fogelman carried her food tray and sat at one of the cafeteria tables.

Chapman laughed. "Olencia that was actually a compliment he gave you."

"What? I thought that meant he wanted enslave me."

"Well, it's actually more that he likes you enough to want to be your man. Enslave, I think, is a little bit of a harsh term. You remember what Lucinda said about their relationships."

"Well, that might be true, Lois. But I also remember what our briefing said before the conflict began about Praxton."

Chapman lowered her voice. "Tell me, do you really believe everything the Charter of Conduct Office says?"

"Good point." Fogelman took a drink of her tea. "But it does seem like a barbaric society."

"Maybe a little. But my husband Jason asked me to pick up souvenirs from Praxton." She rolled her eyes. "You know the type he was referring to."

"Collars and restraints...?"

"Yeah. He said it would be interesting for me to wear them in the privacy of our place."

"I'll bet he would find it interesting. Men...I know my husband finds it alluring too, his eyes bugged out during the newscasts of the Praxton fashions. So what did you tell Jason?"

Chapman was quiet for a few seconds. "I told him to forget it at the time. But, you know, I just might do a little shopping."

"Really? Like a collar?"

"Some of them are quite fashionable on Alliance worlds. So I'd consider a collar. Maybe with those matching cuffs."

"I like those Praxton shoes and dresses. I would like to have an excuse to wear something like that."

"With a collar...?"

"Maybe, I don't know. I want to, but I don't know what others would think."

"No one has to know but you, me and your husband."

"Oh great, then I would be a closet slave." She laughed.

Chapter Eighteen

Diane's elbows were cuffed with a short chain securing them together behind her back. Her hands waved helplessly by her side and she lifted and dropped herself on LeBlanc's erect cock as he rested on his back. Occasionally, he reached up and squeezed her breasts, getting a louder moan from her. Other than the elbow cuffs and her collar, she was naked as she worked to satisfy first him and then herself.

It was when he was in the middle of his climax that his mobile chirped excitedly, signifying an important diplomatic call. He ignored it for another minute and finally he reached past Diane to retrieve the phone that was sitting on the night table.

Diane listened to his side of the conversation as she shifted her hips over him. He hung up and then closed his eyes.

"Good news?"

"Yes, negotiations have started again. I will be hosting talks here."

She grinned. "That is wonderful news."

"Indeed. They requested you attend as well." He opened his eyes and stared at her. "You will have to decide just which side of the table you will be sitting."

"I suppose I might disappoint some people."

He nodded. "Do you need to return to your suite to get your reports?"

"I was thinking more along the lines that I want to stay here tonight and that you should chain me to the bed. I don't feel I can represent the Charter's position any longer."

He smiled. "I like your choice. Yes, I would like to chain you to my bed as well."

* * * *

Diane approach LeBlanc in his office as he worked on various details for the forthcoming meetings. "Master Troy, may I ask for a favour?"

"Of course." He stopped working and turned his attention to her.

"I have been asked to attend the meetings as a consultant for the Praxton delegation."

"That is wonderful news. They will benefit from your expertise."

"Thank you. But I was wondering if I may take a key along to unlock my collar if I should need to do so. I know how politics work and I suspect I will be under scrutiny. Someone may state that I'm proof that females are slaves. I need to refute that."

"Certainly. It is not unusual for females to carry a key for emergencies or when shopping for new collars and outfits that need the removal of the restraints. Thank you for asking for permission first."

* * * *

The meeting room was filled with officials representing different factions. The Alliance worlds' delegation included members of the Alliance government, the Charter of Conduct Office and the Alliance military forces. Ambassador LeBlanc sat with them and looked across from the round table and gave a small grin to Diane Fulton who sat with the group representing Praxton. Her role was strictly as a consultant, but she had been invited to attend because of her knowledge of the Charter of Conduct. Some of the Alliance delegation expressed surprised when she entered the room wearing Praxton fashions, including collar and cuffs.

Ambassador LeBlanc was in an awkward position of being involved with her while sitting on the Alliance government side. However, he was restricted to being the host for the meeting without official input to the negotiations. His superiors were outraged when they found that his interest in restraints and Praxton society had gone far beyond what they considered slight deviant behaviour. The Alliance government was more tolerant than the Charter of Conduct Office on its officials expressing individual views but the Ambassador had crossed the line. Unfortunately, for the Alliance government, it did not have anyone who could step in and conduct the meetings on Praxton soil. It sent LeBlanc a carefully worded message that failure to help Praxton sign the Charter of Conduct would mean his dismissal from the diplomatic ranks. However, a signed agreement might mean simply a transfer to a less controversial location.

During the meeting, Diane was able to bring forward details of the wording and intent of the Charter of Conduct that supported the Praxton position. After a period of heated exchange on Praxton females being forced to wear collars through social pressure, Diane interjected. "That social pressure is no different than the social pressure on most women, and men as well, on Alliance worlds to adhere to fashion trends. On several Alliance worlds, it is now fashionable to wear collars and cuffs. I believe that these negotiations can proceed better if we look at the collars and associated jewellery as fashions rather than as restrictions on females."

She looked at an Alliance negotiator who was preparing to speak a rebuttal. "Please note I'm wearing a collar. I can remove it right now if you want me to show I can do so. I challenge anyone at this table who believes I'm not wearing this collar and cuffs because I choose to do so. Does anyone seriously believe I'm not strong enough to do what I want when it comes to wearing fashions?"

Silence continued for several seconds. Finally the chairman spoke.

"I believe you have made your point, Ms. Fulton. Shall we proceed to the next topic?"

* * * *

Terri took off her shoes as she entered the front door with Romie. Alex Greggory had invited them over to discuss the latest development with Corporal Eric Winston.

She was almost knocked over by the onrushing Allison, who hugged and kissed her.

"I missed you so much!"

"I missed you too, Allison."

Romie laughed. "I thought Terri was my female."

Allison looked worried for a second. "I'm sorry, I didn't mean to…"

Romie waved his hand at her. "That's quite all right. You two go and catch up."

Terri went with Allison to the recreation room while Romie shook hands with Alex.

"I saw your video, Terri, well actually a whole bunch of times. You look really good in that video with Black Steel."

"Thanks. It was a lot of fun doing it."

They sat with several other females, those that lived in Alex's home, plus those that were under the protection of Lieutenant Gallagher.

"So, tell us what Black Steel was really like."

"Well during the video he's aggressive, just like you see. But outside of the video, he's actually very quiet and reserved, not like his screen personality at all."

"You sure looked aroused at the end of that video."

Terri covered her face with a hand. "I was really aroused. We were supposed to stop when he kissed me, but the director yelled for us to keep going. So he kept working me over and suddenly I knew I didn't have any resistance to anything he wanted to do. Then I'm lying on my back and I saw he had this huge erection which just made my mind go numb."

"What did Master Romie say? Did he see it?"

"He was there. He just told me my acting was really good." She laughed. "I'm glad he understood."

The viewscreen in the room was switched to a newscast. A reporter was standing in front of the Alliance embassy with several other reporters in the background still trying to get information from the delegation leaving the embassy. The reporter stared into the camera and spoke.

"As you can see behind me the peace meetings have been recessed until tomorrow morning. While there have not been any comments from those at the meeting, there has been a prepared statement. The Alliance forces have agreed to exchange all prisoners of war. There will be further negotiations on all other matters, and both parties are optimistic a resolution can be found. One interesting sideline is Diane Fulton. The former Charter of Conduct Office representative, resigned her position just yesterday and now is sitting as a consultant for Praxton."

Terri reacted with surprise. "Diane Fulton! That is the woman who tried to convince me to go back to the Alliance worlds. I can't believe she's on our side now."

"You must have done a good job selling there."

Terri laughed. "Sure, I'll take the credit."

Allison pushed her hand higher on Terri's thigh, going slightly under the hemline of the short skirt.

Terri turned and kissed her. "Allison, I can't stay tonight. I'm just visiting while Master Romie talks to Master Alex."

"Darn. It's been a while since you stayed overnight."

"I know. But there will be other times in the future."

"All right. By the way, do you think Master Romie would be interested in being the guardian to another female? The six females staying with us were freelancers, but it looks like most of them want a guardian now. Master Alex has said he's willing to consider taking one or two, but there are others who want a guardian."

Terri was quiet for several seconds. "I don't know." Terri felt her stomach tighten. Unlike most guardians, Romie only had Terri as a female. She didn't like the thought of sharing him with another female.

"That's one of the things Master Alex may be talking to Master Romie about."

Terri was quiet for the rest of the evening, and when Romie indicated it was time to go, she jumped up and said quick goodbyes to Allison and the others.

They walked back home and as soon as they had left Alex's property Terri asked Romie about the other females.

"Are you going to have another female in the household?"

"I haven't decided yet. It is a difficult situation for Alex to take care of all those females."

"I know this is being selfish, but I don't want to share you with another female, Master Romie."

"If I do take one or more females understand that I'm doing so out of being fair to Alex and the females, not because I'm dissatisfied in any way with you."

"I understand. I still want to be your only female."

Romie put his arm around her waist and gave her a hug. "Let me put it this way. I'm likely going to take two females into the household, but not necessarily as their guardian. I feel I should be giving them a place to stay. I'll make a decision later about what capacity they will be staying with us, and that may include me as their guardian. But I would like to talk to you about something else. Two things actually."

"What are they?"

"You still have to complete the course that was part of your immigration requirements. I want you to investigate the various institutions where you would like to take the course. Obviously, I want you to choose one of the top places, money is not a concern."

"Yes, I guess I had forgotten about that. There was something else?"

"Yes there is. I don't need you to answer this right away. But I would like you to accept the Affinity Ceremony with me."

Terri turned and wrapped her arms around his neck. "Yes! Yes! Yes!"

Romie gasped, "I said you could think about it."

"I don't need to. The answer is yes." She kissed him long and hard on his lips.

Chapter Nineteen

Lois Chapman escorted Lucinda Taylor to the infirmary level again. This time she took her without a guard. The rest of Lucinda's cell mates had already left for Praxton, but she wanted to stay until Eric Winston was ready to go back.

"I can hardly wait to see him again."

"Well, you're going to see him lots now. He is being discharged, and I've arranged for you to take him back to Praxton territory."

"Thank you. You have been very nice to me, letting me visit him earlier."

"The Alliance forces are not interested in causing hardships to the people of Praxton. Understand that we only came here to help your world."

Lucinda covered her mouth with her hand, holding back a laugh. "Is that a rehearsed speech? You don't really believe that do you? I like you. You seem really smart and have a kind heart. But that speech doesn't sound like you at all."

Lois held back a smile of her own. "Okay, I'll admit we're supposed to reinforce that we came here to help Praxton. But I do hope the arrival of Alliance forces will be a catalyst for change. Despite your feelings and the argument you made earlier, females on Praxton are not treated fairly under your laws."

Lucinda was quiet for a minute before she responded. "You're partially right. Females on Praxton don't enjoy the same rights as males. But changes are occurring, laws are being reviewed. The people on Praxton don't like lots of change, laws change very slowly because that's the way we like it. Then the Alliance worlds came in with the Charter of Conduct and want us to change overnight. You're trying to force us to change faster than we want to and that's wrong."

"Even if it's for the good of Praxton...?"

"That's arrogance, to assume Alliance worlds know what's best for Praxton. Like I said before, Praxton is changing, but we want to do so at our pace. The only thing that changes fast here is fashion."

"Okay, I see your point. But sometimes a person, a government or a whole world needs to have a shake-up now and then." Lois pointed at the nursing station. "I think that's Eric in the wheelchair."

"It is!" Lucinda increased the speed of her walk.

Lois laughed at Lucinda's excitement. She wasn't sure what she saw in Eric, other than he was a big, good looking man. The nursing staff had found him assertive and a bit condescending towards them.

Lucinda gave Eric several kisses as he sat in the motorized wheelchair.

Lois stood close by and looked at the nursing staff that was clustered near the desk watching Lucinda and Eric. She walked over to one of the nurses.

"So are you glad to see him leave?"

The blonde shook her head. "Not really. He was difficult to deal with at first, but we've found some common ground. I think we'll actually miss him."

"So he became mellower?"

"More like he understood us better. He called us freelancers once as if that was an insult, and then later became more respectful when he found most of us had husbands or boyfriends. Mind you, the girls here also began to treat him better. I think one day he got a back massage and two sponge baths. That would make most guys more reasonable."

"Okay, Lucinda," Lois said. "It's time to go to the shuttle."

The nursing staff said goodbye to him and a couple of them gave him a hug and kiss on his cheek. Eric waved goodbye. "If any of you want to come and visit me I'll be happy to put a collar on you."

One of the nurses laughed. "Does that include chains too?"

"Only to the bed. He grinned at them and then powered the wheelchair down the hall.

They took the elevator to the lower levels, to where several shuttles of various sizes waited. Lois walked them to the loading ramp of one of the small shuttles and shook Eric's hand.

"Good luck and I hope you heal quickly."

"Thanks. Your doctor did a good job on me. I'll be fine." He paused, then said, "Tell your doctor friend I'd still like to collar her and give her a spanking."

"I don't know if she'd appreciate that message." Lois laughed.

"I think she would understand. I'm trying to say I think she's alright."

"Okay, I'll explain that to her." She turned to Lucinda. "Good luck."

"Thanks." Lucinda gave Lois a hug and then several pats on her ass. Lois looked surprised.

"Sorry, I forgot you don't know. It's a custom on Praxton for females to pat another female who's a friend on the behind."

"Well that's an interesting custom. Thank you for thinking of me as a friend."

The shuttle landed near the boundary that marked the end of Alliance occupied territory, a two hundred square kilometre area that had the appearance of a space port. Eric and Lucinda left the shuttle with one of the Alliance soldiers. At the boundary, a Praxton female medic waited with a wheelchair.

Lucinda waited until Eric had switched wheelchairs and spoke to him. "You know you haven't even given me a collar yet, but already you're offering to collar those Alliance females."

"I was just joking." He gave her smile. "But if you're feeling jealous, I could give you more attention by way of a spanking."

"You're in a wheelchair."

"That won't save you." He suddenly grabbed her wrist with his hand and pulled her towards him.

"Okay, okay. I get it."

"I hope so." He continued to pull her to the side of the wheelchair and forced her to bend over.

"Please, Master Eric. I'm sorry."

He reached over and lifted up her skirt. "How sorry?"

"Very sorry, Master Eric..."

He smacked her cheeks several times and then released her. "Now remember this—it's you I'm going to collar. Don't worry about other females."

"Okay, I won't." She rubbed her cheeks. "Ouch." She turned to the female medic who was watching with an amused expression. "I don't think he's going to need much medical attention. Me, I may have trouble sitting for the next little while."

Chapter Twenty

Nicole sat on Lloyd's lap as they watched the viewscreen in Alex's house. Several other people crowded into the room as well to listen to the latest reports from the meeting between the Alliance forces and Praxton.

"Some of the details are yet to be worked out, but as it stands now, some key points have been agreed on. Praxton government has agreed to adopt the Charter of Conduct with the provision that collars, cuffs and various restraints will be considered fashion accessories. There will be clauses added that will stipulate the use of other Praxton unique devices. For example, whips will be regulated as to weight and size of the strands.

"Contrary to earlier expectations, the Praxton government is not going to join the Alliance worlds as a member, but will instead push for new trading agreements. That hinges on the Alliance worlds being allowed to tax some luxury items purchased in the Praxton tourist zone, such as youth enhancement drugs.

"None of these changes will happen overnight. It is believed the Praxton government has three years to adopt and implement most of the Charter of Conduct regulations and clauses."

Nicole breathed out a sigh of relieve. "That's a bit of good news. Looks like Praxton will get to keep its identity."

"Good news for you, otherwise I'd have to squeeze in all your future spankings in a few days."

"The trouble is you like spanking my butt a little too much."

"The real trouble is you like being spanked and find ways to earn them."

She laughed. "We make a great pair that way. You like to spank and I like to be spanked. But not hard, you understand?"

"That's not for you to decide."

Allison came into room looking excited. "Guess what? Terri and Master Romie are going to have the Affinity Ceremony!"

Angela grinned at Allison's enthusiasm. "Did they set a date yet?"

"No, not yet. She's going to need a lot of help planning and asked me if I could give some advice."

"We'll all help her. It should be fun putting it together."

Allison continued to grin. "I can hardly wait to get started on it."

Cassandra spoke up. "Does Terri even have a clue what the ceremony is about? Does she know about being stripped naked in front of everyone and then getting roped?"

Allison thought a moment. "You know she also mentioned she was going to be taking a course on being a Praxton female. I think she's going to be in for quite a surprise in the both the course and the Affinity Ceremony."

About the Author

Nick Howard lives near Grande Prairie, Alberta where winter is never far away. There he pursues a dream of writing and taming weeds on an acreage. So far the weeds are winning but perhaps the writing will allow him to feel a small measure of victory.

He shares the green jungle with his wife, and a dog that thinks itself as human. Rumors that the dog assists him in writing are greatly exaggerated, as the dog is horrible at grammar.

Nick invites readers to email him with their views at nshwrd@yahoo.ca He also has a website at www.nshwoward.com, which has other books and a few free stories. Please be warned the website is intended for adults, so please close one eye if you are sensitive to ladies in delicate situations.

One last thing, thank you for reading this story, and I do hope you enjoyed it.

Other works by the author with Melange Books, LLC

Praxton Series
Slaves of the Rogue World
The Battle For Freedom
The Proposal
A Vote For Change

Novels
Haven
The Witch and the Hairbrush